A Day of Rain

LGBT Short Stories

A.J. Hughes

Love-LovePublishing—Madison, WI
ISBN: 978-1-7334454-2-9
Library of Congress Control Number: 2020937144
Title: A Day of Rain
Author: A.J. Hughes
Digital distribution | 2020
Paperback | 2020

Second Edition | 2022

Cover Art by Maryna Kriuchenko

Also Written by A.J. Hughes

A Walk on the Other Side

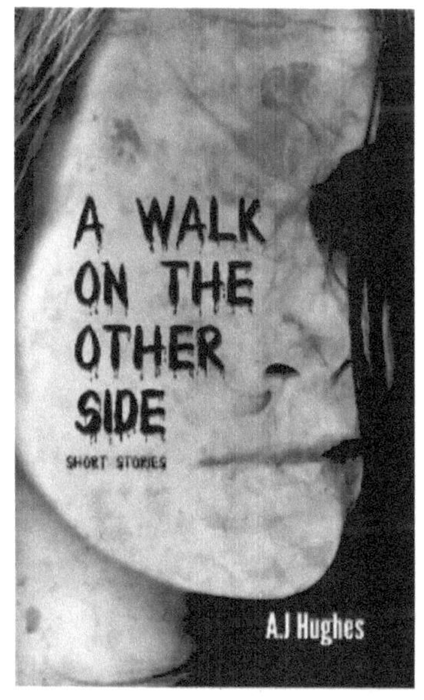

Are you ready to take a walk on the other side? Be prepared for the supernatural...thrillers, fantasies, and tales of ghosts, fairies, and even death. These creepy stories are surely to die for. But not before getting weird. Or just weirded out.

Dedication

I would like to thank my family for all their support. And my mother for being my inspiration to write. Whenever I feel down, I can always count on her to pick me back up. She is my fan and my biggest critic for my work, and I thank her dearly for that.

Table of Contents

Chapter 1

Rain poured down in sheets. The streets were flooded and the trees tilted and swayed. This was the worst rain Wyatt had ever seen. He walked through the downpour alone, feeling like his heart had been ripped out of his chest. He was just rejected. What made it worse, was the fact his first love was a boy.

Wyatt went to an all boys' school and lived in the dorms. He had no family or friends, he was bullied regularly, his grades were terrible, and he just ruined the most peace his life had in so long. Everything was wrong. He had no reason to live.

Why go back to a life of misery, to that school where no one liked him? To a family who didn't love him? To a world where he felt he didn't belong.

Wyatt walked. He walked until he reached the bridge just above the river. He stood there contemplating whether or not he should jump.

"Would anyone miss me if I died?" Wyatt thought as he put one foot over the ledge. It was slippery. One wrong move and he would be gone. He felt a rush of fear. "What's beyond this world? Would I disappear? Would I become an incorporeal spirit floating through this world? Would I have thoughts? Or would I go to Heaven?"

Wyatt walked off the bridge. He felt guilty, despicable. He wasn't even worthy of death. His heart heavy, overflowing with guilt and self-loathing. He stumbled away from the railing, gripping his chest. Wyatt cried. Why couldn't he do anything right?

Wyatt took his time walking back to the dorm. He knew what was waiting for him when he got back. He was worried his crush told everyone. He was the only person that didn't bully Wyatt. He was perfect. He had a lot of friends, he was good at sports and school, and he had a loving home to return to. Wyatt was nothing compared to him. So, what made him think he had a chance?

Wyatt got back to the dorms at midnight. He knew that less people were awake. He entered the building. His mind was crazed. His heart pounded. The entrance was small, but once into the living room or "hangout room," it was huge.

The floor and walls were carpet, the color was tan blue. There was a TV in the corner to the left diagonal to the entrance. The couch was in front of the TV and the loveseat was between the couch and TV to the right. There was a pool table to the right and a table for board games. The stairs were a few feet behind the couch. Wyatt walked to the stairs. He heard some students in the hall above. He wondered if it was safe or worth it. He could sleep outside, in the gym, or the cabin. He did it before. He was out late and fell into the mud. Not only was he muddy, he looked like he had wet himself. And the hangout room was full of all the douche bags that enjoyed picking on him. It wasn't worth it. So he found a building for the night.

But today was different. He didn't want to sleep in the cabin. Not to mention the rain had gotten worse. Wyatt took a deep breath and went up the stairs. He was scared. What if it was Jake and his lackeys? What if it was HIM? Which was worse? Wyatt reached the top. He looked to where the sound came from and saw Carter, one of Jakes friends. Carter looked to his right and saw Wyatt. A devious smile came across his face.

"Well, look what we have here," Carter said. "It's our doggy."

"Great," Wyatt thought.

He turned and began to speed walk to his room. He hurried down the hall, as Jake and his friends followed, calling out names. He was close, just two doors down when Rock grabbed his arm and threw him to the ground. Carter was about to kick him when Jake stopped him. Instead of hitting him, Jake sat on him. His eyes squinted, the look of hate on his face.

"Tell me," he said leaning close to Wyatt's face. "Since, when were you a homo?"

"Oh crap," Wyatt thought. "He did tell everyone. But why? Why did he feel the need to?"

"No, I'm not," Wyatt said wondering if they noticed his voice trembling. "I don't know where you heard that from."

Jake stared emotionless at Wyatt. Wyatt was quivering. Questioning what was going to happen to him. Jake bit his lip, stood up and turned to walk away. Wyatt was relieved that Jake wasn't going to do anything, Wyatt let out a huge sigh of relief.

Jake stopped. As Wyatt was turning to get on his knees to stand, Jake spun around and kicked Wyatt in the stomach. Wyatt let out a gasp. The pain was unbearable. They all joined in and began kicking Wyatt. It lasted for 5 minutes. They knew students were looking through the peep holes to see. But no one cared. Maybe it would have been different if it was someone else? Anyone but him.

When it was over they walked away laughing. Wyatt stood up in pain. It was hard to walk, every step brought pain to his sides. But he needed to get to his room. Away from those eyes. Wyatt walked into the seclusion of his own room. He was by himself. No one wanted to share a dorm with him. Anyone who moved in, left immediately.

The room was dark, the only light was from outside. He walked slowly to his bed. His mind was blank, but he wanted to cry. He lay in his bed and curled underneath the blanket.

It was quiet, the sound of the rain hitting the roof and window filled the room. He cried. Thinking whether it would have been better if he did jump off the bridge. As he lay there, he could hear the commotion from in the hallway. They were laughing at him. Why was he born? Why couldn't he have been born into a loving family? And had friends and life just wasn't this hard?

Wyatt fell asleep.

~~~

Wyatt walked into the classroom. It was his first day of school. He didn't know what to do. He wondered whether an all boys' school was just like any other school. He glanced across the room. Everyone was staring. How could he introduce himself if everyone was staring? He looked to his feet and said his name. When it was all over, his eyes lowered, and he walked to his seat. As the day went on, no one talked to him. His first day was a failure. Just when he thought that, he came. His name was Dylan.

"Hey, you're the new kid right," he asked. "I'm Dylan."

"Hey, I'm Wyatt."

At the time everything was normal. He didn't have feelings for him. They were just friends. But as the days went by his feelings began to show. He started avoiding him. And at the same time Jake set off to ruin his life. As soon as Wyatt and Dylan stopped talking everyone removed Wyatt from existence.

He became a nobody. But at the same time, he kept Dylan in his thoughts. He sat behind him and was his group partner. He wished he could talk to him. Each day he thought of ways to speak to him, but in the end, he could never pull
~~~

it off. The way Dylan stared at him was painful, maybe he hated him for abandoning their friendship. For never speaking to him. What Wyatt felt was real. How could he tell the person he loved that he wanted to be near him? Of course not in a romantic way. They were both guys. He was afraid of rejection. What would happen? That moment of embarrassment would be hurtful. There was no way it would be anything more than a friendship. His heart was broken, he had no way to communicate his feelings. Wyatt had so many chances to tell him but they were gone. He quit the class because he was afraid of what would happen if he stayed near him. He was ashamed, he gave the excuse the class was a waste of time. That there was no chance he could ever take it seriously.

He had no motivation, and no friends to help console him. He started to realize that all of his roommates were changing rooms because of him. He never questioned it, he just assumed they hated the location of the room. So far away from the stairs or their friends. During Christmas when everyone was going home, he had to stay because his family cut off all communication. At first, he thought it was bad timing. But as time went on, the letters he sent weren't replied to, his phone calls were ignored, and his allowance was shortened to an amount where he was close to not having food money. Wyatt had given up. He came to the conclusion that he was not meant to live. Or that everyone didn't care if he died. He got desperate for a friend.

On that rainy day, he was trapped in the library. The rain was scary.

"What are the chances of me getting hit by lightning?" Wyatt worried looking out the window. The field was vast and there were no trees or anything taller for the lightning to strike instead of him. He sat there for hours contemplating. He heard a sound from behind. He flinched and saw Dylan coming from behind a bookshelf.

"Man, will this rain ever stop?" Dylan said stretching. He walked to Wyatt and sat down in the seat across from him. "So you're waiting out the rain too huh?"

"Yeah," said Wyatt. "How long have you been here?"

He had no idea what to do, he hadn't talked to him in so long, he wasn't ready.

"Yeah, I fell asleep," Dylan said pointing back to where he came from.

"Ah."

Awkward silence.

Wyatt was freaking out. How could he be so close? His mind was wondering to places unknown and a will came over him.

"This is my chance," Wyatt thought.

He was excited everything was going well like in his fantasies. Trapped in a room, only the two of them. There was no way this could go wrong. He felt that burst of confidence that nothing could falter.

"Um…" Wyatt said. "I love you."

"What?"

Wyatt hadn't thought this through. Of course in his fantasies he was gonna get the person he loved. There was no turning back.

"I like you. I have since we became friends."

What was he supposed to do? He couldn't take it back now. How could he? What kind of joke would that be? He held the last bit of hope he had and continued.

"I-If there's a possible chance you feel the same, would you go out with me?"

There was silence. Wyatt was scared of what was going to happen.

"You know something?" Dylan said, a smile crossing his face.

"What?" Wyatt asked his heart pounding.

He began to smile. This was the moment. This was the moment when everything up 'til now would matter. A moment when his love would be worth something. A moment that would decide whether he was living.

"This is really…" he paused. "Disgusting."

Wyatt jerked, he thought, "What did he say?"

The smile on his face lowered.

"The fact that you could sit here and say the gross shit, makes you repulsive."

Dylan stood up and left, the door slamming behind him.

Wyatt was abandoned. Left alone with his thoughts. He sat there fighting back the tears in his eyes.

"Was this the right thing to do? Could things have gone better if I hadn't said anything? Would our friendship be back?"

He felt like he was going to drop dead.

"Repulsive" raced through his head.

"Why did this happen?" Wyatt had no way to understand why he was so unfortunate. His life was going downhill. Silently, he cried, so no one could hear him.

Wyatt stood up from his chair, he was dizzy. The room was spinning, and his head hurt. He walked out the library and into the school hall. He walked down the hallway, past his classroom where a person stood staring out the window. He looked at the person, the figure was a blur.

"Is that Jake?" he thought. "No, it couldn't be. He would be beating the life out of me right now."

The figure just stared, his eyes fixated on Wyatt. Wyatt turned and kept walking, passed the main office and out the door. He continued walking. He walked through the field and onto his own secret path. Through a field of flowers being destroyed by the rain. He went forward. Passed the abandoned cabin, passed the tree where he ate lunch, passed the tiny stream where he enjoyed watching things float by. Passed the cherry blossom trees where he read books and sometimes napped. He walked down the street, and to the bridge where he considered whether he should die.

Chapter 2

Wyatt woke to the sound of thunder.

"A dream," Wyatt thought, he sighed and turned to his side.

It was still dark out. Wyatt turned on the light. He wondered what time it was. He looked at the clock. It was 10:30 AM. He was late for class. It was so dark that it looked like the sun was destroyed.

Wyatt jumped out of bed and took his pajamas off. His body had bruises all over, and his brown skin was discolored in some areas. He sighed and put on his uniform. It was black, with red linings. Stitched on the left side of the chest was a sapphire blue and turquoise badge that had the letters EC. EC stood for Emerald Crest high school. It was a very slimming suit even for Wyatt.

Wyatt combed his hair and brushed his teeth. Instead of sharing a bathroom with the entire dorm, Wyatt installed his own to not have to associate with them. He took a deep breath and stepped out of his dorm. His body was still in pain from last night's beating. Wyatt was shocked. People were still there and in their pajamas. He wanted to know why but could not find it in himself to ask. He turned around and started to go back into the room, but he needed to know. He turned around and walked to someone who was alone. He thought that would be better, since they liked to front when their friends were around.

"Hey," he hesitated. "Why is everyone still here?"

"What? Are you deaf?"

"No, I just woke up."

"Ha! Must have been great to sleep with all this thunder," The boy snorted but continued. "Classes were canceled because the storm's too dangerous."

Wyatt didn't know what to say. His question was answered. They had no reason to speak. And it was clear he didn't want to talk to him.

"Thanks," Wyatt said.

The boy mumbled something.

Wyatt turned around without looking at him and went back into his room. The halls were quieting and empty. They probably went to the hangout room. He took off his uniform, put on some shorts and a shirt. It was getting a little cold, so he lay in bed. He stared at the ceiling for a few minutes then closed his eyes. He loved the sound of rain. It was soothing and beautiful.

Wyatt began to doze off when he heard a knock on the door.

Wyatt jolted up and looked at the door. He never had someone visit his room. He walked to the door a little eager to see who. Maybe he was going to make a friend. He looked out the peep hole. Wyatt couldn't believe his eyes. It was the last person Wyatt expected to be there. Jake. Fear rose up and he became still. What was he supposed to do? He backed away from the door as silent as he could.

"I know you're in there," Jake banged on the door. "I swear, if you don't open this door, I'll beat the shit out of you when I see you later."

Wyatt stopped and came back to the door.

"Promise you won't hit me?" Wyatt asked his hand on the lock.

"Yeah, yeah, whatever, just open up."

Wyatt paused and unlocked the door.

Jake opened the door and locked it behind him. That really made Wyatt nervous.

"So, why are you here?" Wyatt said, trying so hard not to sound uncomfortable since Jake decided to only wear underwear.

Jake wasn't an unattractive person. He was rather gorgeous. His hair was short, and his eyes were blue. He was tall and rather built. Wyatt looked at his muscles, they were toned. They weren't too big, but he still had something. More than Wyatt anyway. If Emerald Crest was coed, he would have been popular with the girls. His smile was a sure example of it. If it weren't for his bullying, Wyatt would have fallen for him too.

"No reason. They're all being pussies right now. So I came over here. No one to hang with."

"Ah."

There it was again, he was the last choice, but Wyatt should have been grateful. It was unexpected that Jake would even go near him without physical violence.

Wyatt was exhausted. He sat down on the bed and took a peek at Jake who was spinning in Wyatt's office chair. They sat there in silence until Jake finally spoke.

"Do you have any games?" Jake asked searching through his drawers.

"What do you mean?" Wyatt caught on.

"That was stupid," he thought.

"Are you stupid? Do you know what games are?"

"Yeah, I know. I wasn't thinking."

"Hmm, so do you?"

"No. I only read books."

Jake looked around the room, the shelves held books and in the corners, were stacks.

"You must have a lot of time," he said in awe.

"Yeah, I don't have friends, so I have lots of time."

Wyatt gave a faint smile, his eyes lowered. Jake stood up and sat next to Wyatt his eyes not leaving his. He rested his hand on Wyatt's thigh.

"What are you doing?" Wyatt was flushed.

"Shh," Jake whispered slowly sliding his hand up and down Wyatt's thigh.

Jake carefully and slowly moved his hand up Wyatt's thigh and into his shirt. It felt good. Wyatt was trying not to enjoy the sensation. His face was completely red. He was trying his hardest to suppress his moan. It was getting bad, he was excited.

Jake used his free hand to cradle Wyatt's face as he went in for a kiss. It was a deep passionate kiss that swept Wyatt away. Jake took off Wyatt's shirt and he paused.

"I'm sorry about yesterday and giving you these bruises. Are you still hurt?" Jake looked genuinely worried.

Wyatt shook his head, "No I'm fine."

That was a lie. Even moving a little brought pain.

"Thank goodness," he said with a look of relief.

He kissed the bruise that was on Wyatt's shoulder.

"Why is this happening?" he thought.

Jake mounted on top of Wyatt. This was going too far. Jake began kissing his neck, while his hand groped Wyatt's chest. His touch was soft. Jake gently moved his hands down Wyatt's waist and began pulling off his underwear. Wyatt lost all will to keep calm. His suppressed moans were coming out. Wyatt was embarrassed.

"Why am I the only one naked?"

"Do you want me naked too?"

Wyatt blushed. Was he seriously going through with this? And to top it off, with his bully? It was inexplicable. Why he would even consent to this was something most people would never understand. It could've been because he was so lonely anyone would do or because he craved human affection. Physical touch. Something humans needed. He was just rejected, the only interactions he had at school were in class assignments or when he was bullied… unfortunately by the same person sharing his bed.

Wyatt nodded slightly. Jake got up and took his underwear off. Wyatt hadn't thought this through. He just confirmed that he wanted to do it. Jake went back on Wyatt and kissed his neck. He kissed the bruises on his chest, then back to his neck. Wyatt felt good. Though he wasn't fully aware of the situation. Maybe it was a dream? Wyatt gasped as Jake nibbled his ear.

Jake lifted Wyatt's legs, taking the next step. It was painful but good.

The thought that something like this would happen to Wyatt was a mystery.

Wyatt woke up, it was still raining. Wyatt groaned, his back hurt. He heard the shuffle of his sheets. He forgot Jake was still there. He was asleep next to him. They were obviously cuddling. Wyatt could not believe that Jake was gay. Not to mention attracted to the person he beat up every day. What was Wyatt supposed to say? Did this mean they were going out? These thoughts rushed through his head. Why? Why did he treat him that way? Was this just a joke? Some way to hurt him? Maybe he wasn't gay and just need some "company." Wyatt didn't want to be hurt. He had no idea what to do.

Wyatt got out of bed and took a shower. As he sat there, the water rushing down his face, he felt guilty. Even though Dylan had rejected him he still loved him, and he betrayed that love by sleeping with Jake. He was empty inside. Only a hollow shell by the time he got out. He looked at Jake who was sleep and felt a sharp pain in his chest. He got dressed. He wore a black hoodie with a white skull on the back and black jeans. He grabbed his umbrella and left the room. He locked the door after him so Jake wouldn't be embarrassed. The halls were still clear. How could these teenage boys be afraid of a little thunder? He looked around and when he got to the stairs, he found out where everyone was. Almost everyone was in the hangout room. It was even hard to get down the last four steps because they were infested with boys. He weaved through the crowd of boys sitting across the floor and walked out the door.

Everyone who saw him watched him as he left into the storm that canceled classes that were only 20 ft. away. But like Wyatt said, they didn't care. As he walked through the second door, he was pelted with rain and wind. Debris was everywhere. Why would he go out into this?

The rain was deadly. But he kept going. As he walked through the school field the wind started to pick up and threw his umbrella. He ran through the field of flowers that were no longer there, and to the cabin. It was his shelter, his way of getting away from everything. He had what he needed. Inside there was a warm bed and blanket, there was a couch and beanie, there was a cooler for food, a kitchen, there were 5 shelves full of his favorite books, a fireplace, a working toilet, and a window to watch the rain fall. Wyatt was at peace, secluded in that cabin with the rain outside making a beautiful sound. When he was there, he could really believe his life was worth something. That he had a home, a place to return to. He didn't have to think of where his family would be, or that he was harassed at school. That was where he was supposed to be.

Wyatt grabbed some firewood and started a fire. He rested on the couch curled in his blanket with one of his favorite books, Autumn Leaves. He stayed for hours, despite the fact that he had no clock to see the time, and it was dark out since morning. Wyatt closed his eyes and took a deep breath. He read 10 books and was tired. He crawled off the couch and into bed. He closed his eyes.

Not long after, he heard something tapping on the window. It was Jake. Why was he there? No one was supposed to know about his secret world. He wanted to ignore him, but he had compassion. He knew it was bad out and Jake was soaked. Wyatt got out of bed and opened the door. Jake walked in his face red and shivering. Wyatt brought a towel for him.

"Thanks," Jake said.

"How did you know I was here?"

"I saw you leave from your window."

"Oh, well hurry up and dry off. So, you can quickly leave," Wyatt walked back to his bed and lay underneath the covers.

Jake walked to the bed and lay down next to Wyatt. Wyatt could feel him staring.

"Why do you want me to leave?" Jake inquired his hand lightly touching Wyatt.

"Because this is my home. Where I want to be alone," Wyatt whispered.

"Well for today maybe you can be alone with me," Jake said his voice low and sweet.

Wyatt said nothing. He wondered why he wanted to be near a loser. He stayed quiet and pretended to sleep. Jake slid under the blanket and held Wyatt.

"He's cold," Wyatt thought.

His face turned red and he moved in closer. He heard Jake give a soft chuckle and squeezed him tighter.

~~~
~~~

Wyatt recalled the time they first met. Jake was staring at him from across the room. Wyatt had no idea what to do, so he smiled. Jake looked away quickly and continued his work. It was the first time he made contact, even before Wyatt met Dylan. How could he not remember that until now? Jake would always sit next to him, but Wyatt would move to sit with Dylan. He was oblivious to Jake's advances. Why didn't Wyatt ever tell Dylan to sit where he was sitting? If that had been the case, maybe he would have acknowledged Jake and fallen for him instead. Would he not be so unhappy now? It seemed as though Jake wanted to be friends with Wyatt, to become closer. Maybe that was why he became a dick, and ONLY harassed Wyatt. Wyatt blushed and looked up at Jake who was looking out the window.

"He's actually kind of good looking when he's not smoking, or bulling me," Wyatt thought. Embarrassed, he looked back down and closed his eyes.

As they lay there, the sound of the rain hit the roof and Wyatt could hear the beating of a heart.

Chapter 3

It was the next morning but there was no sign the rain would stop. Wyatt stared out the cabin window. He and Jake had a peaceful night when they heard lightning strike a tree. They heard a huge thud, the tree dropped in front of the door. It was just their luck. They were in the middle of a field unknown to the school or any other person. They were going to be stuck for days and Wyatt only had a set amount of food for one person. With two it would go out sooner. Wyatt sighed. Just when things were making a turn in his life, he got stuck. While Wyatt was wallowing in his depression, Jake was in the kitchen making breakfast. Wyatt heard a sizzle and smelled burnt eggs. He jumped and ran into the kitchen. Wyatt looked at Jake who had no idea what he was doing.

"Hey," Jake said. "I made breakfast…or what was supposed to be anyways."

Wyatt looked at the pan, and sighed, "It's better than nothing."

Jake smiled and placed the eggs on plates. They sat down to eat. Wyatt was nervous for some reason. He couldn't explain why he was so cautious of Jake. Maybe it was because his bully was eating breakfast with him, or because Jake was his first. But he was curious why he would like him. And since when.

Wyatt hesitated before asking, "Do you like me?"

Jake stopped eating and stared before saying, "Of course, I wouldn't have slept with you if I didn't."

"Then why did you bully me?"

"I don't know. I was mad you didn't like me. That you were straight. And some part of me knew you were gay. But I knew if you were, you liked Dylan."

Wyatt jolted with the mention of Dylan. "W-what do you mean?"

"I overheard you in the library. Honestly, that was super bogus of him to turn you down like that. Even if being gay is uncomfortable to some guys, that was too harsh. Crushed my heart listening."

"So he didn't tell everyone I asked him out?"

"Probably not." Jake shrugged. "I didn't hear anyone talking about you."

Wyatt was relieved Dylan didn't say anything. Grateful, he looked down at his plate and stirred the eggs.

"H-how long have you liked me?"

"Since you transferred," Jake quickly responded. "I kept trying to get close to you, but you ditched me every time. So I bullied you cause you rejected me."

"That's not an excuse," Wyatt mumbled poking the eggs.

"I know, and I feel really shitty about it. I'm sorry."

Wyatt was a forgiving person and decided to let it go. "I'll except it if you promise to stop bullying me."

"Obviously." Jake flicked his forehead. "We're dating right? I wouldn't… couldn't be mean."

"But you were before," Wyatt said.

"Because I'm petty," Jake said taking a huge bite of eggs.

Wyatt smiled. "I forgive you."

Jake smiled back and kissed Wyatt on the forehead. "Thank you."

They embraced once more.

Everything began to change for Wyatt once they left the cabin. Of course, not everything was solved overnight. But in the coming months,

Wyatt was finally living a normal high school life.

A Day of Rain

I didn't know who I was until I met you.

The Library

I was in a committed relationship with James for 5 years. We started dating junior year in high school, and we decided to go to the same college and move in together. He was a sweet guy, he treated me with respect, and genuinely loved me. But something just didn't seem right. I did love him, but over time I lost those feelings. When we graduated high school, I questioned so many things. My mother could sense I wasn't interested in him, but she pressured me to stay with him. I was 22, and this was the prime age to find someone to settle down with. I would be losing something special and could end up with the wrong person, or never finding someone again. Constantly fearing what she said, I stuck with James. But on just one rainy day, everything changed. I remembered it, as if it happened yesterday.

It was a Friday morning, and there was a terrible rainstorm. I needed to get to class, so I went out despite what James said. I could barely walk, the wind was so strong. My glasses were slipping off and my lenses fogged up. I gave up and went into the first building I could find.

I took my glasses off and wiped my lenses with my drenched shirt. I looked up to see where I was, the room was blurry, but I could make out books. I was in a bookstore or maybe a library. I knew it wasn't the public library, that was on the other side of town. So maybe a private one?

I heard a gasp, "You're soaked. Let me get you a towel or something. I might have something lying around."

She shuffled through her drawers and in bins.

"Ah ha," she shouted raising her arm in the air. "It's a shirt, but that's better than nothing right?"

I took the shirt and said, "Thank you."

"No problem," she responded. "You're crazy to go out in this weather. This is hurricane weather."

"I know, but I needed to go to class. My professor doesn't cancel class for anything."

"If he doesn't cancel for this, he's an asshole. As you can tell, it's actually pretty dangerous outside."

"Yeah," I laughed. "I haven't seen this place before, is this a bookstore?"

"No, it's my private library, but I let people in to read the books."

"This is your own collection?" I shouted.

"Pretty impressive huh," she said proudly.

"It definitely is. I always wanted to start my own library. I didn't think it was possible though."

"It is, you just can't get government funding, and generally a private library is for a select few. So it wouldn't be open to everyone."

"I didn't know that," I said looking around at the aisles of books.

"Well I have to get back to some work. You're more than welcome to sit and read any books you want."

"Thank you," I said smiling. "Oh wait, I don't know your name."

"Angel," she said.

"I'm Hannah."

"It's a pleasure to meet you."

Angel went back to her desk and began typing. I watched her for a little bit, before turning to look at the books. I didn't even know where to start. I walked to the first shelf of books. Thankfully everything was labelled. I walked to the middle aisle and walked alongside the shelves. Reading each label until I came across the graphic novel and manga section. It was like

I really was in Heaven. I went down the first row and came across the Shojo manga or "girls manga" as it translates to. She had everything labelled by genre. She really was amazing. I wondered if she did this all by herself or if she had help. She even had BL and GL, boy's love and girl's love. She was very open. I went back to the Shojo manga. And picked up one of my favorite series. I never got to finish reading it, the last few volumes were extremely difficult to find, or you would be paying $200 for one book. I walked to a lounge area I saw walking through the aisle and sat down.

Angel walked to the back and was shocked to see me still reading.

"You're still here," she said sitting down.

"Oh yeah, I found a lot of books I wanted to read for years."

"I'm glad you found them. And I'm definitely glad I came back here, otherwise you would have been locked in here," she said laughing.

"Oh are you closing?"

"I planned to. It's already 6."

"Wait really?" I asked looking at my phone.

Time escaped me and before I knew it, it was 6pm. I was so enveloped in these books I didn't even realize it was dark out.

"I'm sorry, I didn't even notice."

"It's okay," Angel said. "I'm glad you like my selections."

I stood up, "I should get going so you can go home."

"Either way," she said. "We can talk longer if you want."

I sat back down. We talked for hours. James called a few times, but I ignored him. It was interesting finding out about her. Her family was rich, but she invested a lot of her allowance or inheritance on her library. She was 27. She was the youngest out of two girls and one son. She was supposed to enter an arranged marriage with her father's business partner's son, but she turned it down. Her dad was pissed but she didn't care. They didn't know each other. She wasn't even going to inherit his company, so why would she do something like that. Everything was fine with his business partner, but he was still angry with her. It was the principle, that she would defy him.

She said there was more to the story, but she didn't want to delve deeper. I learned about her favorite genres to read, her favorite genres of music were classical and pop. We had a lot of things in common. I loved talking with her. Maybe it was because I was so used to conversations with James, I enjoyed the change of pace. Getting away from the same dull conversations.

Angel looked at the clock on the wall and said, "It's almost midnight. I really should get going."

"Yeah," I said. I almost mentioned James, but for some reason I didn't want her to know about him.

We walked slowly to the entrance, still talking. After Angel locked the doors, she said, "It was a pleasure talking to you."

"I'll come back tomorrow, if that's okay."

"Of course it is," she said.

Angel reached over and hugged me. My heart was beating really fast. It felt nice, I couldn't necessarily explain how I felt then, but I didn't want to let go.

Angel let go and said, "I'll see you tomorrow."

"Yeah," I managed to let out.

I waved as she walked in the other direction.

When I got home, James was waiting on the couch.

"Where were you?" he asked.

"I was at a library. Why?" I asked taking off my shoes.

"I called you so many times, you couldn't pick up once?"

"Oh, I'm sorry. I had my phone on silence."

"But you could have answered."

"Again, I was in a library," I said harshly. "What did you need?"

"Nothing, I was worried about where you were, you left out early this morning in a bad storm. You never told me you went somewhere safe. I assumed something bad must have happened. You could have called at any time and let me know you were okay."

"I didn't think about it, I just got encased in what I was reading. I didn't even know what time it was."

"Yeah, but you never seem to make me a priority."

"Where is this coming from?" I asked

"Maybe because of the fact, you're coming in at midnight. I didn't even get to spend the day with you."

"We spend every day together. I can go out and enjoy some time by myself without your permission."

"I never said you needed my permission. I just want you to communicate more with me. I had no idea where you were."

"Whatever," I said walking out of the room. "I had a wonderful day. I don't want to deal with your negativity."

"You can have a wonderful day, but at the expense of my day."

I ignored him and closed my room door. We slept in the same bed, but I had a separate room to study and relax in when I needed time alone. I heard James slam the other room door and I rolled my eyes. Lately, we were getting into more and more arguments, usually started by him. I was just done with it. I already fell out of love with him, but our arguments were making me start to hate him.

I wanted to leave him so much, I desperately needed to get out of there. But when I called my mom and told her my plan, she refused to let me go back home. She genuinely believed he was perfect for me. And did not want me to mess everything up. I didn't have anywhere to go if I did leave him. I never made close enough friends because me and James were always together. My sister lived on the other side of the country and my brother in France. I couldn't afford a plane ticket. So I was stuck with him until I could find a place of my own.

The next day, I went back to Angel's library.
"You actually came back," she said astonished.
"Of course, I never go back on my word."

Angel smiled. Her smile was contagious and made me smile too. Before I could say anything, my stomach growled. I was embarrassed. Angel laughed. She could see how embarrassed I was.

"There's a bakery across the street, do you want to go there and get some food?"

"Sure," I said unable to get over what just happened.

We talked as we crossed the street and into the bakery. Everyone looked weirded out as I ordered. Angel wasn't hungry. I was wondering why everyone was so alarmed by us being there. I just ignored them and ate with Angel. As I finished my sandwich, Angel asked if there was anywhere I wanted to go?

"Not really," I said. "I mean I have to get some new shoes, but I just buy whatever."

"I can see that," she said looking at my shoes. "Let's go down the street to that strip mall and buy you some shoes."

"Okay," I said.

I had a lot of fun picking out shoes with her. She made something I thought was so boring fun. I really owed her for that. After I was done shopping, we went back to her library and talked for hours again.

Over the next few weeks, I visited Angel after class. I would tell James I was going to the library to study more. And he was nice enough to let me go alone, sometimes. Other times, we argued because he just couldn't stand spending time away from me. I always made sure to come home no later than 8pm so we could spend time together but that just wasn't enough for him. Going to Angel's library was my escape from a toxic relationship. When we talked, I forgot about the arguments I had with James and I was whisked away to my own nirvana. A nirvana with Angel. I couldn't express how I felt about Angel. She was so sweet and cool. She was beautiful and mature. The majority of the time, our discussions were sophisticated, but we could also be goofy together. Angel gave me something James could never give. Peace when I was with her and longing when we were away.

James could tell something was different about me. Whenever I let him know I was leaving, he would badger me to tell him where I was really going. Angel let me take books home. When he needed proof I was at the library I pulled out one of her books. He was apologetic at first, but then he became indignant even though he was wrong.

James took me by surprise one day. I kissed him goodbye as I was leaving to the library.

"You know something," he said.

"What?"

"All this time, I really thought you were going to the library."

"I am, where else would I go?" I chuckled nervously, something about him was off.

"Really?" he asked. "Because you said you were going to the library yesterday, but I went there, and I didn't see you."

"Which one?"

"The only one we have in town," he shouted.

"You're wrong," I said quickly. "I go to a private library because there's too many people at the public library. They're too loud."

"Do you actually expect me to believe you?"

"Yes," I snarked. "Why would I need to lie to you?"

"I don't know why. But you are."

"Look," I whispered. Noticing the staring eyes on campus. "I'm not going to argue with you right now. If you think I'm lying fine, but I'm going to the PRIVATE library I go to. You can just deal with it."

James rolled his eyes and mumbled, "Good luck getting into the house tonight."

"Excuse me?"

"Nothing," he said walking away.

I was so annoyed with him I didn't even want to see Angel. Not like how I was feeling. I didn't want her to see me angry. I followed behind James, he hadn't noticed until we were halfway home.

"Where are you going now?" he said stopping to wait for me.

"Home," I said walking pass him.

"Not going to the library?"

"No, you pissed me off too much. I don't even think I can focus on studying."

James grabbed my arm and pulled me to him, "I'm really sorry for how I was acting. My friends have been getting in my head telling me you're cheating on me. When I went to the library and didn't see you, I was angry and sad. Then to top it off you came in at midnight, so that only raised my suspicions."

James leaned in to kiss me, and I turned my face, so he kissed my cheek.

"It's okay," I mumbled. "I don't blame you. I would be suspicious too if this were reversed. I'm sorry, I really am going to a library to study. My friend owns it, and she only lets her friends in. Sometimes random people, but that's why I can stay there until late at night."

"That makes sense," he said. "Have I met her?"

"No," I said. "She's older than us."

"How much?"

"She's 27."

"Oh, that's not bad. But she owns her own library. That's pretty impressive."

"Isn't?" I said getting excited. "She's living the dream I had when we were younger."

"You wanted to own a library? You never told me that."

"You never asked," I said smiling.

We walked home holding hands, I realized I didn't hate him. Just because I wasn't in love with him, didn't mean I needed to despise him. He was a great person to have as a friend. We spent that night just talking about what we wanted to do and what we dreamt of doing.

The next day, I didn't go to class. I went to Angel's library.

"You're here," Angel said looking at me from her desk. "Don't you have class?"

"I do, but I told my professor I was sick."

"You shouldn't skip class."

"I normally don't but I'm just not in the mood to go. I would rather hang out here."

"Aww, that's very sweet," Angel said. "I have to work, so I can't talk right now, but you can go ahead and read."

"Okay," I said.

I walked to the graphic novels and grabbed a comic. I wasn't much for comic books, but I didn't want to finish all the manga she had. I went back to the couch I sat in daily and took my backpack off. As I did, I could see Angel working steadily at her desk. I smiled and sat down. I really wanted to talk but I didn't want to bother her. I leaned back and read the comic.

I opened my eyes and saw Angel leaning over me.

"Finally awake?" she asked.

"I'm sorry, I didn't mean to fall asleep."

"It's alright," she said shaking her head. "It can get pretty comfy in here. A lot of people have done it."

"I don't feel as bad now I guess," I laughed.

I looked at my phone, it was 2pm. I was stunned I slept so long. I looked down to see 3 missed calls and 5 texts from James. I rolled my eyes and sat my phone down.

"What?" Angel asked smiling.

"What? Oh nothing, it's just my boyfriend is being obnoxious."

"You have a boyfriend?"

"Unfortunately yeah," I said. I regretted saying I did but I couldn't tell why.

"Unfortunately?" she repeated. "Normally you're supposed to say you're dating someone in a positive way."

"I know, but I don't want to be with him."

"Then why don't you just break up?"

"I won't have a place to go. My mother refuses to let me go back home because she doesn't want me to break up with him. She thinks he's the right person for me, but I haven't loved him in years."

"Years, wow. That's crazy your mom isn't being supportive of you but of your relationship with him."

"Yeah, I wanted to break it off so many times, but she would tell me things that would make me scared to leave him. Or make me feel pressured."

"How long have you been with him?"

"5 years. And half of it, I didn't love him."

"You should really leave if it's not for you. No matter what your mom says, just get out of there."

"I wish it were that easy. We live together and I can guarantee he wouldn't just let me stay there after breaking up. Nor do I want to have to deal with whatever happens afterwards."

"Well, if you're comfortable with me, you can stay at my place. But you would need to end it with him. It's not fair to him, if you're in this relationship and don't even love him. And it's also not fair for you to force yourself to stay with him, for his sake or your mother's."

I didn't say anything and just nodded. She was right, this whole time, I wasn't being fair to James or myself by staying in this relationship. I wasn't giving him the chance to find someone who would love him, and I was forcing myself to stay with someone I didn't love. My mother wasn't right, it would take time to find that person that loved me, but I wouldn't be alone forever.

After some time I said, "You're right. And I would like to stay with you, but I don't want to be a bother."

"Then you should go home now and talk to him. I'll wait here for you."

I said goodbye to Angel and headed home. James was lying on the couch watching tv. I took a deep breath and walked fully inside.

"Hey, I wasn't expecting you to come home so early," he said sitting up.

"I know, but we need to talk."

"About what?"

I sat down next to him and took his hands.

"I don't know how to do this," I said avoiding eye contact.

"Uh oh," he said jokingly. "I think I know where this is going."

I looked him in the eyes, "I want to break up."

"I figured," he said nodding. "I'm surprised we lasted this long."

"What do you mean?"

"I noticed we were growing apart years ago. But I could tell you were really trying to make us work. Then you started going to your friend's library and we grew even further apart."

He continued, "I always had a sneaking suspicion you didn't love me anymore. So I was always mentally preparing myself for it."

"I'm sorry," I said.

"It's okay, really. I want to be honest too. I started having feelings for someone else too. She hangs out with my friends' girlfriends, and she's also single. So when they would invite us out, and you couldn't make it. It was always me and Jenny as a pair."

"So you cheated on me?" I said.

"Of course not," he said defensively.

"I know," I laughed. "I'm just joking. Besides, I can't be too much of a hypocrite, I think I'm starting to like someone also, if I haven't already fallen for them."

"Really? Who?"

"Angel..." I said nervously.

"Your friend?" he said taken aback. "A girl."

"Yeah, shocking right? I didn't suspect it either. But with her, I feel like a part of me that was missing, is complete now."

"Well, I guess you cheated emotionally first."

"What? No, we were just friends. You went on dates with 'Jenny.'"

"They weren't dates first off, and secondly, you're the one who snuck off coming home late every night after being with her."

"You have a point…"

We both laughed. James seemed fine. We both had found someone else.

"I hope we can still be friends," I said.

"Oh obviously," he said. "We've been together for 5 years and that doesn't include how long we've known each other. Don't you think it would be weird if we just stopped talking?"

"Yeah."

"And we can stay roommates. If you're comfortable still being here, we can just chill like this, for a while. Until we're ready to move in with our partners."

"Yeah, we can do that. I was going to stay with Angel if things didn't go right. But I'll just tell her tonight, I'll stay with you."

I stood up, "She doesn't know I like her, and she might not even find women attractive, but you never know."

"Good luck then," he said. As I opened the door James said, "Wait. So are you lesbian? Or is it just her?"

"That's a good question," I replied. "To be frank, I don't even know myself. It would explain many things if I were, but at the same time, I was in love with you for like 3 years."

"I mean, you can still love someone regardless of their gender. They're the only one you love before going back to your sexual preference. I don't know. I could have been your exception. I was your first relationship, so you never know."

"Yeah you're right. Thanks James, I'll see you tonight then."

"Yep, later."

I closed the door and took a deep breath. It felt like a huge weight had been lifted off my chest. I had Angel to thank for that. I walked down the steps, the air was crisp and fresh.

I walked as fast as I could to Angel's library, I practically ran there. I turned the corner and saw a rundown alley.

"What?" I said. "Did I make a wrong turn?"

I looked around, everything else looked the same. I knew I was in the right spot. I looked at the bakery Angel and I ate at, the shoe store she helped me buy stylish shoes, so where was her library? She must have been pulling a prank on me. She had enough money to make this alley, or a fake street that resembled the real thing. I paced around the blocks. But every time I came back around, it was only the alley. It was getting dark. I walked to a park and sat down.

"No way," I said to myself. "It really isn't there. Then what was happening the past few weeks? Where was I really? Was Angel real? Or did I just look crazy?"

My face tightened as I tried to hold my tears in. I stood up, there were too many people in the park for me to just start crying. I walked, I didn't know where I was going, I just let my feet take me wherever. I walked past the alley, passed the bakery and shoe store, over a bridge and into a dense forest. I didn't care, I just kept going. I stopped when the sidewalk ended.

In front of me was a burned down building. Flowers were recently placed there, and a framed photo. I crouched down and looked at it. My mouth dropped when I saw the face of the girl in the picture. It was Angel. Underneath her photo, was an article:

April 19, 1998

Angel Jones, daughter of Willie and Angela Jones, owners of Jones Pharmaceuticals, dies in fire at the old library on the edge of town. The Jones' did not give us any comments on how and why she was there. But after speaking to her friends, we learned Angel wanted to own her own library and was planning to start renovations. The cause of the fire is unknown, but fire fighters suspect the furnace exploded or a tipped candle setting fire to the books. Nothing remains of the building. Angel was loved by everyone and will be missed dearly. May she rest in peace.

"Angel died in 1998," I mumbled. "Wait."

I looked at the article again, "Nothing remains of the building." I looked up and saw the build was still intact. It was bright red, and the garden and bushes were alive and well taken care of. I was confused and a little freaked out. Did someone rebuild it or something? I sat the frame down and stood up. I had a feeling, telling me to go inside the building. I opened the gate and walked down the path to the building. When I reached the door, I paused. My heart was racing. Angel must have been a ghost. But what was I seeing right in front of me? Tears swelled in my eyes, I inhaled and closed my eyes. As I exhaled, I opened the door.

"Welcome," Angel said sitting at her desk.

The inside resembled the library in town. I glanced around and looked back to Angel. I didn't say anything.

"You're probably confused," she said. "No, you are confused."

I nodded.

She sighed, "I don't know where to begin. The day you met me, was the anniversary of my death. I was given the chance to have a library just for a little while. But no one would come far out here and see it. So I found that abandoned alley and managed to create this over there. But no one could see the shop. So I was discouraged. But then you came in, drenched. I was confused as to how you could see me and all of this."

Angel raised her arms and moved her arm pointing from one side of the building to the other.

Angel continued, "I was so thrilled I could be a librarian. I pretended like I had some work to do. It got really boring and you weren't leaving, so I went over to talk to you. I never expected you to come back again and again. But by the third day, my time was up. I didn't want to leave you. I enjoyed talking with you. I'm not supposed to talk about how the afterlife works, but I can say it gets lonely. Talking with you brought back what it felt like to be alive."

"Why didn't you just tell me what was happening? The truth?"

"I'm not allowed to talk about that, otherwise I have to leave the human world," she said. "But they kept telling me, my time was up and that I had to leave but I just couldn't disappear on you. I asked them if there was something I could do so I could stay by your side a little longer."

"What did you have to do?" I asked.

"Be your guardian Angel temporarily. They explained what was wrong and said if I can help you overcome your problems, I could stay here. But only in this library, and only for you. But I couldn't do it."

"But you did help me," I said. "You helped me break up with James, you gave me a place where I felt I belonged, you helped me…"

I paused, I didn't want to say that she helped me realize all this time, what was wrong, and why being with James wasn't right. I was lesbian and I loved her.

"I had a time limit," she shook her head. "I know I helped you figure out who you were, and helped you speak up to James. But my time was up long before that. I didn't want to talk about your boyfriend. That was the worst possible thing for me."

"Why?"

"Isn't it obvious how we feel about each other? I already knew you were dating him. You weren't open enough to tell me, and I didn't want to hear you say it. But my stubbornness was what screwed this all over."

Angel placed her head on her desk. Her curly hair fell softly, "I'm really sorry."

"It's not your fault," I said walking around the desk to sit next to her. "I should have been honest too and said it. How much time do we have together?"

"Not long," she said. She looked at the clock, "When the small hand hits 9."

"That's in 10 minutes," I shouted. "We have to do something memorable, so we never regret it."

Angel sat up and looked at me. My face turned red. She really was stunning. Angel leaned over and kissed me passionately. Her kiss took my breath away. Angel pulled apart and hugged me. I wrapped my arms around her waist, closed my eyes and hugged her tightly.

"Thank you for everything. For making my dream of a library come true. Thank you for reminding me what it felt like to be human. Thank you for loving me."

"Thank you too, if it weren't for you, I would still be stuck in a relationship with James and be very unhappy. I would have never known who I was."

Angel's warmth slowly dimmed, and my arms went into my lap. Angel was gone. I opened my eyes to a dark room. A lit path led me to the door. I gripped the handle tightly and turned the knob. As the door opened, the once vibrant green grass and colorful garden were gone. And all that was left was moss covered dirt. I closed the door and walked down the steps, down the path and to the broken gate. I turned around one more time, the building was gone and all that remained was blackened ash and rubble. The frame by the gate was covered in dirt and cracked. I picked it up and held it close to my chest.

"If it's alright Angel," I whispered. "I'm going to take this home with m—"

I couldn't even finish speaking. I burst into tears and dropped to the ground. Hugging her photo, I cried. I would never forget her, and I could never stop loving her.

"I love you," I repeated over and over as tears streamed down my face.

Ame no Hi

雨の日

—A Day of Rain—

"I like you; I have since we first met."

Small and frail looking, his smooth skin, innocence look, egotistical attitude, all things about this man I hated. To look at him would be to look at the stars…yeah he's that beautiful it's corny. At first glance you'd think a girl, except for his "manhood." Which consisted of the fact that he wore a male uniform, had short hair and way too many ear piercings, and most importantly no boobs. So why was the most popular kid in this all male boarding school asking me out?

This day COULDN'T get any worse.

The New Kid

You're probably a little confused, so maybe it's best I start from the beginning.

It was a Thursday morning. I was looking at the storm brewing outside my classroom window. The class was dark and dreary, the walls blue and the tiled floors were black. The class was as noisy as always until our teacher came in with a boy. He looked so careless and indifferent.

"Students! Take your seats, please," Mrs. Dragan said. "As you all can see, we have a new student. Go on, tell them your name."

Mrs. Dragan was a petite, round woman with an ill-tempered attitude. Only thing that was good on her was her you-know-what…. If you don't get it, I meant her hair.

"Aww he's so cute," said a classmate.

"Yeah, I just want to eat him up!"

He seemed like he would fit in great here, just by his looks alone.

"Go on," she beckoned him.

He said nothing but looked out the window next to him.

"Well aren't you the silent type," Mrs. Dragan groaned with frustration. "Tell the class your name, or do you want detention on your first day?"

"..."

I wondered what his problem was.

"I swear if you don't tell them your darn name, you'll wish you were at your old school."

With a sigh, he finally said, "Seijirou."

His voice soft and quiet.

"What?"

"That's my name, 'Seijirou,'" he said, taking a quick glance around the class, then back toward the window.

"Really what's with him and windows? Maybe it's a fetish?" I thought.

"Well, 'Seijirou' take a seat next to Michael," she pointed at me, with a smirk. She really did not like me.

He said nothing but walked to the window seat next to me.

"Hey," I said, catching his attention. "I'm Michael. Nice to meet ya. If you need anything don't hesitate to ask."

Again, he said nothing, but shifted his eyes back to the window.

That was the first time he pissed me off, like he was too good to say "hi".

As class went on, I found myself looking at him here and there, "He looks like a woman."

I felt awkward to be looking at another man.

"Oh, he fell asleep," I thought when I looked at him, even when sleeping he looked beautiful. I hated people like him so much.

Ding-Doonng.

"Wow, he's so adorable when he's sleeping."

"Yeah, I just want to sit here and watch him sleep."

"Let's take some pics to send to everybody."

My class was stupid. I wondered if I should wake him up. I guessed that would have been the right thing to do. I shook him awake.

Later that day my ex-girlfriend, who broke up with me not too long ago, texted me saying "hi." Why was she talking to me? She broke it off saying she did not know if she loved me, or I her. So, I simply didn't reply. I waited at the bus stop, and you just wouldn't guess who I was delighted to wait with. He came to the bus stop. I really did not want to talk to him. And I'm pretty sure he didn't either.

But to my surprise the child smiled and asked, "What time does the bus come?"

I could have just ignored him, but I would have felt guilty later, "Not too long, about 5 minutes."

"I didn't ask when YOU thought it was going to come, I asked what time it was officially going to come?"

"What a jerk," I thought. "I was doing him a favor and he dared to say that he didn't like my reply?!"

"Well, sorry. Maybe you should ask the bus driver when it comes. You definitely don't NEED my help," I was so annoyed.

"What's your problem," he sneered, rolling his eyes.

"I don't know, why don't you ask your mother?" I wished that bus would come sooner.

It was quiet, that probably hurt him.... NOT THAT I CARED! I don't know what it was about Seijirou, but everything he did pissed me off. I just met the guy, but it felt like I knew him before. And just thinking about it, made me frustrated. Every time I looked at his face, I got angry.

At last after that awkward FIVE minutes, the bus came. He sat down immediately in the front, so I went to the far back.

For some reason, we got off the bus at the same time. We even walked the same way.

"So, do you live over here?" I asked trying to break the tension. "Um, which house?"

"That one."

He pointed over to the house next to mine.

"Oh, we're neighbors huh?"

"Great," I thought. I was so awkward, and mad that the guy I "disliked" was my next-door neighbor.

"So... you wanna come over?" he asked.

That was a surprise.

"Um... well. Why?" I asked.

It was weird, not even 10 minutes before, we were fighting.

"I don't know... I just thought that we should, you know get to know each other first."

"Get to know each other why?" I thought.

"Yeah... I guess you're right," I responded before I could even think.

His house was pretty decent on the inside. It was neat, and the decorations were weird. His walls were red, he had toy birds hanging from the ceiling and walls. The couch was floral roses. The carpet was fuzzy and blue, really not your average house.

"Would you like something to drink?" he asked.

"Uh yeah, anything's fine."

Silence.

"You could go to my room. It's just up the stairs. Turn right and it'll be the door on the far left."

I walked up the stairs, and into his room. It was at least normal. It was a little dirty, cluttered with books. I sat on the floor, right in front of the bed. After waiting about 3 minutes, Seijirou walked into the room with what looked like strawberry Fanta and Doritos.

"Wow, I love strawberry soda."

"I kinda guessed that you would," Seijirou said his face turning bright red.

"Are you ok?" I asked, he looked like he was really gonna blow.

"Yeah! Yeah, totally fine."

"Why is he so nervous?" I thought.

"Um, so. Wanna watch a movie?"

"Sure. I don't care what it is."

"Alright, so Happy Happy Panda Bear? or Mokku Mokku umi Kuma?"

Both were lame.

"Um, Mokku Mokku umi Kuma."

I didn't know how that one ended. Happy Happy Panda ended with the Panda bear getting attacked by sharks that could walk and breathe on land.

After 30 minutes of sheer terror, Seijirou turned off the movie.

"What are you doing?"

"It's boring and you know it."

He was right. But what came next was worse. Seijirou leaned over and kissed me on the lips. For someone his size, he was very strong. I tried to resist.

"S-stop! What are you doing? NO! Mmm," I finally pushed him off. "What the heck's your problem?!"

"I'm sorry. I- I just thought that you wanted that."

"No, I'm not gay," I said getting up.

I stormed out of the house and went to my room. I had no idea what his deal was. He thought I wanted to kiss him? I didn't know how he could have made that assumption. What was even more strange was the fact I reacted to his advance. I lay on the bed and closed my eyes.

My face was hot, and my chest began to ache. Why was I feeling this way? My head was throbbing, I really felt like I was forgetting something. I buried my face into my pillow. I needed to forget what happened.

The next morning was fine. I kept to myself and Seijirou to his. We barely interacted unless we had to. I tried my best not to make eye contact.

That whole day was just getting worse. No matter where I went it was always about Seijirou. "Oh, did you hear? Seiji likes pickled plum flavored candy."

Or, "Oh my gosh, Seiji spoke to me. He said, 'Excuse me.'"

I swear, that was why I hated people. I'm not the type to just slack-off and not take good care of my grades. I'm a plain, serious and successful person.

During lunch, Seijirou fell asleep again. I wanted to crush his good rest and go on my way. But as I was making my attempt someone more terrible than *him* came in. *Ryuichi*. He was in junior high, but for some dumb reason he kept coming to the high school.

"Is that him?! Isn't he supposed to be with the first years? Why's he here?" Ryuichi said, walking toward us.

Ryuichi was also someone who the entire school favored. That was part of the reason no one kicked him out. Ryuichi was a dick. My relationship with him was bad from the start. It was my first semester in high school, and his in junior high. I accidently bumped into him and before I could apologize, he started dogging me. I was rude for not saying "sorry," he even went the extra length to spread a rumor I was gay.

"Hey! Wake up," Ryuichi said shaking Seijirou.

"Leave me alone," Seijirou waved him off.

"Who do you think you are?" Ryuichi replied grabbing a water bottle and pouring it on Seijirou.

"What is with these two and their anger issues?" I thought.

The water soaked Seijirou. Everyone was shocked. Seijirou flew up, flinging water everywhere and ran out the door.

At the time it was nothing more than a mere gesture of kindness. My body moved before I could even think. I grabbed my bag and left the room to find Seijirou.

"Great," I thought. "I guess that means I have to go help. He couldn't have gotten THAT far."

I searched the halls for him, looking in empty classrooms and bathrooms. Eventually I came to the abandoned hall where many stories were told. Just before I entered the room, I got a text from my ex May.

I'm sorry to say this, but I regret our breakup and I want to get back together. May—

We weren't even broken up a week and she wanted me back?

"What type of BS is that?"

I replied, *Let me think about it*— and that was that.

I walked into the room, it was dark and dirty. The wooden floor was cluttered with old instruments and chairs. Just by looking at the old cello full of cobwebs and old broken music stands near the door, that room hadn't been used in years.

"Seijirou?" I said, the lightning outside illuminated the room. "Come out. There's no use crying over spilled milk…or in your case spilled water."

I heard a little rustle on the right and there I saw him. His small, thin body hunched over crying in a corner. My heart began to ache, and my head started throbbing again. I wanted to see him smile.

"Hey," I said touching his back softly. "Why are you crying over something so irrelevant? Ryuichi is like that with everyone. Not to mention he's a spoiled child."

"I know who he is," he mumbled. "Ryuichi is my younger brother. He hates me for something I had no control over."

It was so awkward, I didn't know what to say. I had no idea how to deal with someone else's feelings, "Come on, I have an extra uniform if you want it, it may be a little big but that's okay."

"Why are you helping me?" Seijirou asked, wiping his snot infested nose. "Don't you hate me for being a jerk?"

"Not really, I was just annoyed. Come on, before you catch a cold," as we got up, I noticed that he seemed a little fidgety. "What's wrong?"

"Do you really not remember me?"

I stayed silent. I recognized him, but I didn't know from where.

Seijirou looked down, "I figured you wouldn't."

"Where do you know me from? Are you sure you aren't mistaking me with someone else?"

"No, it's definitely you. Michael Washington," he forced out. "We were best friends in elementary school. You promised to marry me, I never forgot."

"I d-don't remember that," I stuttered. "A-and besides that was in elementary school. That was kid—"

"I like you. I have since we first met," Seijirou interrupted, lightning striking the ground outside.

I was shocked, why was he telling me this? We were both males, it was weird, "Well, uh, what am I supposed to do?"

"I don't know, I didn't think it through. Uh," he was seriously blushing. After a while he finally said, "Will you go out with me?"

"Sorry, I'm going out with my ex-girlfriend she just asked me out not even 5 minutes ago," I probably should have pretended to think about it. "Besides, two guys going out with each other... it's disgusting."

"Crap, I didn't mean to say that," I thought. It wasn't supposed to come out.

"What's so gross about liking another man?" Seiji said, tears rolling down his eyes. I felt that same strange feeling in my heart, at the time I considered it guilt, and nothing more. "You didn't think that when we were younger."

"That was so long ago, people change. And I probably meant it as friends."

"Surely you have some feelings for me, the way you talked and smiled the day we met again. I'm not wrong I just know it."

"Look, I'm sorry. I didn't mean to say that, it slipped out of my mouth. Nor did I mean to give you false hope."

"But that's how you feel, whether you said it or not," Seiji exclaimed, the rain was really coming down.

"I'm sorry."

Silence, I got a text from May saying, *What's your answer?*

"Is that your girlfriend?" Seiji asked.

"Yeah," I was hesitant to tell him, but it was the only thing to ease the atmosphere.

Seiji looked down, a sad look on his face. Slowly the memories of elementary school flooded in, I remembered Seijirou, I remembered Ryuichi, his little brother. I remembered the crush I had on Seiji. His parents divorced and his mother took Seiji and moved away. I was so heartbroken I erased him from my memories.

Suddenly, Seiji flew out of the door, and down the hall. I didn't know why I was worried about him, he was a man and so was I. It would never work out. Even if I loved him as a kid, I kept the excuse that children didn't know anything about sexuality, or what the difference was between a man and woman. But I couldn't help worrying about him. He was obviously going to go out into the storm.

But that was not the issue, I had to stop him, and let him know that there could be a possibility. Whether or not I loved him. I ran out the room.

"Wait!"

He was fast. No matter how much I screamed for him, he just would not stop. We ran outside.

The ground was wet and slippery. Lightning streaking the sky. The sky was red, the clouds dark and gray. It was hard to see. The rain was getting in my eyes. I was close to catching him. But I slipped in a pile of mud. I got up and before I could reach the gate and get to the street, a truck came barreling down the road. It had to be going at least 50 mph. Seijirou flew into the street, his mind was crazed. Tears streamed from his eyes making it harder to see. The truck driver blew his horn, but Seiji did not listen. He kept running. You have no idea how much I was going crazy to stop him. If I had known this was going to happen I would have said yes or not answered his question at all. The truck had reached him, I began to cry.

"Seiji! Watch out!" I screamed running even faster. I tried my best to save him. But before I could push him out of the way, the truck was there…

I knew I loved him, but it was too late.

A Night of Rain

A Peaceful Night

Max sat by the window watching the rain fall. His thoughts went back to his neighbor Justin. He moved next door about two months ago, and it was love at first sight. He didn't know what it was that he liked, but he felt an attachment to him. He smiled when he pictured the look on Justin's face when he introduced himself.

"I wish I could talk to you," he said burying his face in his arms.

Suddenly, Max heard a loud ruckus at Justin's. He looked out the window to see Justin's dad throwing him and his things outside.

"I don't ever want to see you again," he yelled before slamming the door.

Justin wiped the mud off his clothes and grabbed his belongings. Max watched as he stood there pacing in a circle, his hands on his head. Justin looked up and saw Max. Max flinched and closed the curtains.

"He saw me," Max thought. "What do I do?"

Max wondered if he should let Justin in, it was cold and raining. His family was out of the country for a month, so it wouldn't have been a problem.

Max nodded and headed downstairs. He opened the door as Justin was walking toward the street.

"Justin," he shouted. He ran over to Justin with an umbrella. "Are you okay? If you want, you can stay at my place for a while."

"Is it cool with your parents?"

"They're out of town visiting my older sister, they won't be back for a few weeks."

"Are you sure?" he asked.

"Yeah, we have a guest room you can stay in."

Max grabbed Justin's arm and pulled him inside.

"This is your room for now," Max said his heart pounding.

"Thanks," Justin said putting his bag on the floor.

"Um, if you need anything, I'll be in my room," Max pointed to the sky-blue door across the hall.

"Okay, thanks."

Max closed the door and quietly squealed. He jumped around his room and onto his bed.

"I can't believe I actually talked to him," Max laughed. "Not only that, I get to live with him."

"This day couldn't get any better," he thought.

Max faced the window and looked at the lightning flashing in the distance.

"It's going to thunderstorm soon," he thought turning over.

Max heard a light knocking on the door, "Come in."

Justin opened the door in a tight t-shirt and his boxers, "Mind if I hang with you a bit?"

"Sure," Max blushed.

Justin walked into Max's room and sat on the floor next to the bed.

Max was nervous, it was hard to talk to him. Max didn't know anything about Justin. And he was too shy to randomly say something.

"Argh," Justin yelled.

Max flinched, "Are you okay?"

"Yeah, I just really want to rant about my father."

"You can if you want to."

"Seriously?"

Max nodded.

Justin bit his lip and shook his head, "I don't know. Sometimes you believe you can tell your parents everything, and they say they'll love you no matter what. I told my father I was gay and liked our neighbor. He got so angry he hit me and threw me out. My mother did nothing. I'm alone. If my own parents don't accept me, who would?"

"I would," Max said. "Just because your parents don't, doesn't mean you're alone and no one would accept you. There will always be at least one person on your side. And I'm sure the person you like, likes you too. Your parents moved to a neighborhood with almost all gay kids."

Justin stared at Max, "You're right. There's always someone."

Max looked away from Justin.

"So you said everyone is gay here, does that mean you too?"

Max's heart pounded harder as Justin asked, he nodded and said, "Yeah, my parents found out last year."

"And they still accepted you."

"Yeah, they stand up for LGBT rights, so they loved the fact I was."

"That's nice," Justin said. "Do you like anyone right now?"

Max blushed, "Yeah, I also like someone over here."

"Yeah?" Justin asked raising to the bed. "Is there any chance it's me?"

Max didn't know what to do. Was Justin confirming because he liked him too or was it because Max was too obvious?

"If so," Justin continued. "I'd be really happy."

"What?" Max thought.

"You like me?" Max asked.

"Yeah, that's why I came over to introduce myself. I wanted to get to know you."

"Me too," Max said.

"Well we have until your parents are back to have alone time."

"Why not after?"

"Because I don't think your folks would be okay with a 23-year-old hanging out with their son," he chuckled.

"You're 23?!"

"Yeah, I'm old. Are you going to lose interest in me?"

"No, you're actually younger than me…" Max mumbled.

"I don't believe that," Justin said. "You're in high school."

"No, I'm 25. I just graduated college."

Max showed Justin his diploma and said, "See? I'm the old one."

"Wow, I worried about being a pedophile, but you were actually older. I guess I don't need to hold back," Justin smiled.

Max laughed. He never thought his unrequited love would be returned. And neither did Justin.

Justin leaned over and kissed Max on the cheek, "But not today. Can I sleep in here?"

Max nodded and lay down.

"Good night," Justin said spooning Max.

"Good night."

Max listened to the rain patter on the roof and the low rumbles from thunder that coincided with Justin's light breathing. Max was so happy. His two favorite things were finally together in his room.

A Night of Rain

I loved the rain, but on that rainy spring night, I loathed it with every fiber in my being.

Everything Will Be Okay

T he rain was always my escape from unhappiness. When it rained, I sat in silence and listened to the soothing sound of rain patter on my roof and on the ground. The low rumbles of thunder overlapping the rain and my heart. Any pain I felt, the rain would wash away.

On a spring night in April, the rain became my worst nightmare.

My best friend Alex was transsexual. She hid it from her parents and our peers. When she came to my house, we would play in my mom's makeup. They never thought twice about it, they assumed I was forcing her to wear it because I didn't have any female friends. They didn't realize, she was my only girl friend. We were both there for each other, when I came out to my parents, she was there when I needed her. My parents weren't accepting of it, but they put up with it until I was 18 and they could kick me out.

When Alex came out to her parents, they accepted that she was gay. But Alex didn't have the heart to tell them she was also trans. She knew each thing took time and placing both on her parents would be too much for them to handle. When we were 15, Alex decided she was ready to tell her family she was trans. She wanted to stop wearing male clothing and wanted to wear the dresses I gave her. Her mother understood, but her father was angry. He became belligerent and told her, he got over her being gay, but wanting to be a woman was going overboard. That didn't discourage her from letting her true self out.

The next day, she wore one of the beautiful dresses I got her, I came over early in the morning and helped her with her makeup. When we were done, she looked absolutely stunning. Her mother complimented her, and her father said nothing. He never spoke to her after that. He pretended like she didn't exist. But Alex kept going, she pushed through the backlash. As long as I was there by her side, she could do anything.

Still, even the strongest people suffer. And some don't have a voice to ask for help. Regardless of my support, Alex felt she couldn't tell me everything.

On that rainy night, I received texts from her. I couldn't understand what she was saying. She just kept sending me text messages apologizing. And telling me she couldn't do it any longer. A sense of dread hung over me, as I read her last text.

"She's not going to do what I think she is," I said to myself.

I called her, but she wouldn't pick up.

"Please, please, please pick up," I said again and again as tears streamed down my face.

A text came from her, she apologized again, and told me she couldn't handle the constant stares from our peers and those in our city. She couldn't do it anymore, but she didn't want to hide who she was any longer. She told me goodbye.

I called Alex's mom, and asked where she was. I told her that she was going to commit suicide. I rushed over to Alex's home so she could read my texts. She called the cops to look for her, and she sent me home promising to tell me when they found her.

It was pouring outside, but it couldn't wash away my fear. I paced my room, waiting for Alex to return my texts and calls. The sound of rain pattering on the roof grew more and more agitating. The sound of thunder expressed the darkness that would unfold. I wanted to hear nothing from it.

A few hours later, the rain let up and silently hit my roof. I got a call from Alex's mom, I could hear it clearly as she said it. Alex was dead.

I erupted in tears. I couldn't save her. She was suffering so much. I looked up to her bravery, but little did I know she was hurting under that layer of skin. Every time we laughed at people's reactions to her, Alex was internalizing it. It was all my fault. If I had been there for her, she wouldn't have done it.

It hurt so much losing my best friend. I never told her how I felt about her, she was interested in men, but I loved her for who she was. And I lost her forever. I couldn't see her cries for help. And I was the one who was supposed to be there for her like she was for me.

At the age I am now, I knew it wasn't my fault for what happened, it was societies pressure to put down people that were trans and didn't identify with a gender. But at 17, I couldn't think rationally. I felt alone, my best friend of ten years had just killed herself. She was my shoulder to cry on and I was hers, but she was forever gone.

For years, I could never forgive myself. I spoke to so many helplines, but it wasn't enough. When I turned 30, I met a woman named Riley, she understood how I felt. She lost her girlfriend to suicide. And explained that it wasn't our fault. We supported them as best we could. But sometimes, it takes more than consoling them to help. She told me I shouldn't blame myself for what happened. And that it was okay to move on. Alex wouldn't want me to suffer. And so I did, I moved on. Alex was and is always in my heart. I started a serious relationship with Riley, and we've dated since.

When it rains, it's not soothing. The rain fills my heart with sadness. It pours heavily on my heart as I remember that night.

A Day of Rain

Sweet and kind to everyone. I loved her dearly.

Naomi

Kind to everyone, she was the perfect woman. She was beautiful. When she smiled, the room lit up. It was like her mission was to make everyone's day better. She made sure to compliment everyone she saw. There was no way anyone could hate her. I enjoyed the classes we had together. No one paid attention to me and I usually sat alone. When Naomi was there, she would always sit with me. I felt special.

There was only one problem, she was straight. The likelihood she would ever like me was next to none. And it hurt. I never saw her with a guy, but we were in a small town that didn't condone being lesbian. I was 100 percent sure I was the only gay person in town. It hurt being so close to someone and never being able to tell her how I felt. She might have been uncomfortable if I told her. I wouldn't be able to bear it. My heart shattered just thinking about it.

I planned to move to a city where being gay was accepted, but I just couldn't leave. Naomi was the only thing tying me down to that small rundown town. Each time I mustered the strength to leave, I packed my bags and I book my flight. But when her face popped into my mind, I lost the will to escape.

The only people that knew I was lesbian were my parents and my little brother. When I first came out, my parents weren't very happy, I can say that. But over time, my mother came around. She still loved me, no matter what "faults" I had. I can tell my father still hasn't fully opened to it, but he said he loved me regardless. My brother always suspected it, so he wasn't surprised and didn't care. How he explained it to my parents was, it wasn't his life, so it wasn't his business. If I was or not didn't matter to him, it was my life.

We never got along, but after that, we became closer, and I helped him with his girl issues, and I shared whoever I had a crush on. I kept Naomi a secret. As popular as she was, I felt embarrassed. I was the last person she would ever consider dating. I felt silly thinking about a relationship with her. But each day, seeing her smile, I couldn't help but love her.

I was content. As long as she stayed by my side, I didn't care if we were just friends. I wasn't as close as I wanted to be with her. But in class, she was the center of my world, and I felt like I was the center of hers. Silly thinking, I know, but I loved her so much. The slightest gesture was enough to make me elated. But things were changing fast, and my world crumbled before my feet.

On a rainy day, I came to class drenched. I didn't know it was going to rain, and I thought it would be a perfect day to walk. But it began to pour when I was halfway there. When I entered the classroom, everyone laughed. They really thought I was a loser. I lowered my eyes and went to my table. I wanted Naomi to come and make me forget everything, but at the same time, I didn't want her to see me like this. I couldn't see myself, but I knew I looked a mess. The room was obnoxiously loud, some were still talking about me and the other half talked about whatever obnoxious things college students talked about. I put my head on the table and closed my eyes. I wanted just a moment of peace. And just like I wished, the noise stopped abruptly. I lifted my head a little and saw Bryan, the most popular guy at school, his armed wrapped around Naomi and her head rested on his shoulder. The widest smile on her face, as they entered the room. Naomi never smiled like that with me, not with anyone. My heart sunk into a bottomless pit. It took everything for me to not cry. I wasn't going to do it. Not to myself, not in front of these people, and out myself.

I watched as Naomi followed Bryan to his friends, not even a passing glace my way. The class ruptured into cheers as they sat down. Everyone crowded their table. They asked so many questions, it was all they discussed while we waited for the professor to come. When did they start dating, how long they liked each other, who asked who out? They really made the perfect couple. The two most beloved people now came in a set. I couldn't listen any longer. I took my headphones out of my bag and turned my music on loudly. I lay my head back on the table and closed my eyes. I shouldn't have come that day. I knew she would eventually start dating someone, but deep down, I wished she were lesbian. And I held on to the little bit of hope she would fall for me. And in just one day, that hope was snatched away.

When class was over, I raced out of the room and walked home. I didn't say bye to Naomi like I always did, I couldn't muster up the strength. I would cry the moment I looked at her. I burst through the door, ran to my room and cried. I cried for hours. The day went by and my room grew pitch black. I ran out of tears to cry, and just lay in bed looking into the darkness. The rain silently pattering on the roof and window was soothing, but it made my heartache. I took a deep breath. I just needed to survive another two weeks before the spring semester ended, and I got my liberal arts degree. There was nothing holding me back from leaving now.

The following two weeks, I avoided Naomi, but it didn't really matter. She hadn't even noticed I was avoiding her. All of her attention was on Bryan. She never looked my way, and my heart ached more and more. But I had to push through.

In what seemed like an eternity, it was the last day. It was time for my last final and I was ready to move on.

I walked into class, and everyone was silent. I was so used to them saying something ignorant about me, but they said nothing. I was suspicious and checked my seat to make sure they hadn't done anything. I sat down and opened my textbook to study. I could overhear the group behind me. They were trying to be quiet, but they were louder than ever.

"I still can't believe it," a girl said. "It can't be true...can it?"

"Davis saw them," one of the guys said. "Look at the video again."

I listened to the video and could hear a group of guys shout in shock at something.

"There's no way you can lie your way out of that," the guy continued.

"I just feel bad for Naomi," the other guy said.

"Poor girl," the girl said.

I turned around, I didn't want to talk to them, but I wanted to know what happened to Naomi.

"Uh, if you don't mind me asking," I interrupted. "What happened?"

"You didn't hear," the girl shouted. "Let me see your phone."

The girl moved over to my table and sat down, "Watch this."

I took the phone and watched intensely. There were two people kissing under a bridge. The camera zoomed in and there it was, Bryan kissing Scott, another football jock. My mouth dropped and the girl took the phone.

"Shocking right? Who woulda thought he was gay?" she laughed.

"By now, almost everyone has seen that video."

"Have you seen Naomi?" I asked.

"Not yet, but I hope she's alright if she's seen it yet."

"Yeah, me too," I said. "Thanks for telling me what happened."

"No problem girl."

I turned around and rested my head in my palm. I wish I had Naomi's number, I wanted to make sure she was okay. I sighed and looked back to my textbook. The door opened and everyone's eyes shot to the door. I quickly looked up as Naomi walked in and Bryan behind her. I looked down immediately. They didn't even bother sitting with his friends. Naomi walked over to my table.

"Hey," she let out. "I know I haven't sat with you in a long time, but is it alright if we sit here?"

"Sure," I said not looking at them.

The group behind me, stood up and moved away.

The girl from before, as she sat down said, "If you don't want to sit with him, you can come over here with us."

Naomi smacked her lips and I shook my head, "I'm fine right here. I don't mind sitting with them. Thanks though."

"Thank you," Bryan said.

I smiled and went back to studying. I wanted to direct all of my attention to Naomi, but it was time I got over her. Unrequited love wasn't something worth having anymore. And now that I've seen her with a guy, I know I don't stand a chance with her.

"Are you mad at me?" Naomi asked.

"No," I said shaking my head.

"I feel like you are, I know you are. And I don't blame you. I started dating Bryan and I haven't talked with you since. I'm really sorry."

"It's fine," I forced out.

I really didn't want to hear any more. I clenched my fist tightly around my pencil as she spoke.

"It's really not, and you can pretend you're not angry, but you haven't even looked at me. You're not as attentive as you used to be," she said sitting closer to me. "If there's something I can do to make you forgive me, I'll do anything."

"There's nothing you can do," I said quietly.

I bit my lip. I didn't mean to say that out loud.

"So you really are mad," she said.

I shook my head, "I'm not mad, but you wouldn't understand."

Before she could respond the professor came in apologizing for being late.

"Let's talk after, I'll wait for you if I finish first," Naomi slid her chair back to where it was.

I was so upset over Naomi that I couldn't focus on the exam.

Just as she said, Naomi finished before me and whispered, "I'll wait outside the room."

I didn't know what she wanted to talk about, but I couldn't listen to it. I needed to leave town. And the moment she said what she needed to say, I would give in and stay. I would forever be stuck in a web of unrequited love, in her web and she would never know I was there. Desperately clinging to her for life, until I died never feeling her warmth.

After looking over my exam for the 6th time, I took a deep breath and stood up. Bryan was still there, he looked up at me.

"I understand your feelings," he whispered. "Good luck."

I smiled and said, "Thanks. I wish you the best too."

I handed my test in and walked to the door. I took one last deep breath and walked out the room. I looked for Naomi and didn't see her. My heart dropped further into the pit. I got my hopes up, only to be crushed again. I walked away from the room and turned the corner. And leaning on the wall with her hands behind her back, was Naomi. Shocked, I just stared.

Naomi turned and looked at me, "You took a pretty long time. Was it really that hard?"

"No, I just wanted to make sure I got the answers right."

Naomi giggled, "That's so like you."

I smiled. I missed her laugh, I missed her.

"I really want to apologize," she said becoming serious. "I should have been a better friend, or at least spoken to you, after I started dating Bryan."

"It's okay, really."

"It's not, I didn't even do something as basic as tell you we were a fake couple."

"A fake couple?" I repeated.

"Yeah, Bryan just started dating Scott, but you know the deal, this town isn't very LGBT friendly."

"So you said you would date him, so that no one would suspect him and Scott?"

Naomi nodded, "But as you can see, everything about them is out there, so they want to just be free and start dating publicly. They were both accepted into the same university in Minnesota, so they don't have to worry about people judging them."

"That's good for them," I said. "I was planning on leaving the state too. Finding somewhere more accepting to everyone."

"Really?" Naomi asked, disappointment in her voice.

"Yeah, I don't have to worry about telling you this, since you're open to them. But…" I paused. Even though I knew she was okay with the LGBT community, I was still scared to tell her the truth about me. I took a deep breath. I couldn't hide it anymore. And I didn't want to. "I'm lesbian."

I wanted to say more, but I was too scared. I wanted to tell her I was madly in love with her and have been for years. That every day was torment because I couldn't be with her. That my love for her was driving me insane. But I knew that would make her uncomfortable, I was only her friend. I bit my lip, retreating from my last chance.

Naomi said nothing, she was probably stunned by how random it was.

"I'm sorry," I said. "That obviously made you uncomfortable."

I wanted to run away, as far as possible. My eyes filled with tears, I lowered them and turned around.

"Not at all," Naomi finally spoke. "I'm just shocked because I thought you were straight."

I shook my head as I turned to face her again. My cheeks were burning, I didn't know if it was from finally speaking to her or from how embarrassed I felt.

"So that makes four of us."

"Four of us?" I asked.

"That are gay. Bryan, Scott, you and me," she said smiling.

"Whoa, wait," I said taken aback. I tried my best to keep my voice down, "You're lesbian?"

"Is it that surprising?" she asked.

"Yes, I thought you were straight. So many guys like you and you talk to all of them."

"Well yeah," she said. "As friends. I already have a crush on someone."

"Really?! Who?" I asked.

"Do I need to tell you?" she mumbled looking at the floor.

"Yes, I would really like to know," I said staring intensely at her. My heart was beating so fast.

Naomi paused and huffed. She looked back to me.

"You, of course."

"M-m-me?" I said. My heart was actually racing. I felt like I would have a heart attack.

I couldn't believe it. It must have been a depressing dream. No way this was really happening. I knew I was gonna wake up soon.

"Yeah, I'm glad you're lesbian at least, so I don't have to worry about you being uncomfortable with my sexuality."

"I'm not, it's just... I like you too. And have for years."

"Years," she said. "Why didn't you say something?"

"We live in the most homophobic town. You can't tell who is or isn't homophobic."

"You're right on that," she laughed. "But years, you definitely have me beat. I've liked you for a year, so I'm pretty happy right now."

"Me too," I said.

I was euphoric, it just seemed too good to be true. I didn't know how to respond.

Naomi smiled, "So was that why you avoided me the pass two weeks? Because you really thought I was in love with Bryan?"

"Yeah," I said

"That's sweet, I'm really sorry I didn't tell you. I didn't know if you were an ally or not."

"It's okay," I said.

"Do you really plan on leaving?"

"I want to eventually. I want to go somewhere I'm accepted and I don't have to hide it."

"Why haven't you done it yet?"

"I didn't want to be apart from you."

"Well, if you're okay with it," she said. "I'd like to go with you."

"I'd like that," I said smiling. "We can leave together."

Naomi and I left the school, our hands intertwined. We were leaving anyway. Who cared what any of them thought? We stayed quiet as we walked. Partially because we were a bit nervous at the stares, but also because we were in pure bliss.

"Say," I broke the silence. Something had clicked, "Even though you were dating, you didn't have to avoid me so much. How come you didn't sit with me sometimes?"

"Well," Naomi said smiling.

Her smiled turned into a grin, and she burst into laughter, "It seems silly now, but I...felt kind of guilty for dating Bryan. Like I was cheating on you. Plus, even though the way we came into the class was a big deal, I didn't want you to think we were dating."

"Well, you didn't do a good job hiding it."

"I know," she said.

"Also..." I trailed off.

"What?"

"How come you like me? Like what made you fall for me?"

"It was how attentive you were. Like yeah I'm popular and whatnot," she said. "But something about the way you looked at me, made me feel special."

"Well of course," I said. "Because I liked you."

She laughed again, "Well geez, don't ruin the reason I liked you. I also liked how you didn't let our class bother you. I like how mature you are. What made you like me?"

"Your personality. You're kind, sweet, and pretty, what's not to like."

"You're making me more nervous right now," she laughed covering her mouth.

"Sorry," I said.

We decided to go to my place, her parents didn't know she lesbian. And us showing up hand in hand wouldn't have been pretty. She spent the night, and we talked until morning. I treasured every minute. My feelings were finally returned. Our hearts were finally connected.

Naomi and I moved into an apartment in Brooklyn. We loved the fact we could kiss in public without someone calling us slurs and harassing us. We escaped a town of hate and found our everlasting paradise together.

A Night of Rain

It was never supposed to turn out this way. I wished I never said yes to drinking with him. If only I could turn back time, far back to before I loved him.

Unrequited Love

I was in love with my roommate. But there was no chance of him ever liking me. He was straight, popular with women, and a bit of a homophobe. Whenever he saw or dealt with a gay man, he would always make comments afterwards to me. Comments like, "He was checking me out I could tell. I don't understand why they need to like guys, it's gross." or "Dude, I was freaking out. The guy in the bathroom was definitely gay. He was looking at my dick. I swear every gay guy is after me." And those were the "more appropriate comments."

When I first developed feelings for him, I didn't know he was homophobic. I was open about my sexuality, and everyone on our campus knew. But Jackson asked me to room with him anyways. I figured he was an ally or was gay but after a few months his true personality came out. It was too late for me. I started to like him over little tiny things like complimenting me, laughing, having fun, drinking and his amazing talents. And I know you're wondering why I could like someone like him, but it's hard. It's easy to fall for someone, but losing those feelings was practically impossible. I've tried, don't get me wrong but it seemed like something pulled me back to him every time. We all know someone that has had a bad relationship, you just can't escape it. And after a while, I didn't want to.

It was never supposed to turn out this way. I wished I never said yes to drinking with him. Jackson was in a relationship with a woman named Leah, they were doing it everywhere. From the couch, to the kitchen, the bathroom, you name it. Their relationship was just about sex, and the only person who didn't see it was Jackson. Leah was done. She lost interest in the sex and told him, she wanted to see other people.

In his state of depression, he asked me to get drunk with him. This was a ritual between us. Whenever our heart was broken we went binge drinking. That night, he wanted to stay home so he wouldn't run into her. If I had known what was going to happen I would have said no.

Like usual, we drank, and he ranted over her,

"She's such a bitch," he slurred. "She doesn't know what she's missin'. Bu who cares, bros before hoes ammi right?"

"Definitely, lets cheer to that," I said raising my glass.

A few drinks later, I was barely thinking straight, I couldn't walk. Jackson already gave up on trying to move. So I sat back down, this time right next to him.

"Why are you sittin' so close?" he asked pushing me away. "What are you a fag?"

"And what if I am?" I asked looking him in the eyes. "Would you hate me?"

"Man, this is fuckin' weird," he said. "But I dunno, probably no, you my bro."

My heart skipped a beat, "What did he just say?"

I swallowed and said, "Well have you ever thought about being with a guy?"

"Fuck no," he shouted. "I'm no fag."

"You don't have to be to have sex with one."

"What, you telling me you done it with a guy before?"

"I was really drunk, and a gay guy hit on me, next thing you know we have sex."

"Broo," Jackson said. "What was it like?"

"Weird, but no different than fuckin' a girl."

"Really?" Jackson said. "And it worked?"

"Yeah," I said.

"How, who was the guy and who was the girl? Who went inside who?"

I sighed, "For some reason, I was the bottom."

"BRO," Jackson yelled. "You fuckin' kiddin' me?!"

"Nah, he lunged right on top and stuck it in."

"Where?"

I looked at Jackson for a bit, it took him a minute to realize where.

"Fuck," he said. "Is that even possible?"

"You'd be surprised," I said.

Jackson just nodded and looked away as if trying to process this.

A thought popped in my head, I wish I never said it, but I was too drunk to think.

"You wanna try it?"

"The fuck?" he said looking grossed out.

"You wanted to know what it was like right? I've done it before, so you can see with a straight guy. We never speak of it again."

Jackson paused. He didn't know what to think.

"Let's do it," he said as if coaching a football team.

My heart was pounding. I was really about to go through with this. I swallowed and leaned in to kiss him. It was passionate and I got on top of him. Jackson wrapped his arms around my waist.

"Shit," Jackson said biting his lip as he pulled away. "Drew, you sure about this?"

"I don't know. Only if you are," I said. "We're both drunk I don't want either of us to regret this."

"It'll be our lesson for getting so drunk," Jackson chuckled.

Jackson stopped and looked me in the eye before leaning in again to kiss. I wrapped my arms around him as he lay me on my back.

"I haven't done it with a guy before."

"Obviously," I said. "But you always brag about how you and Leah had anal. It's basically the same."

All Jackson said was, "Oh" as he kissed my neck, then my chest, he was going to continue lower before he hesitated.

I sat up and motioned for Jackson to take his pants off. I looked down and back at Jackson, "Not gay huh?" I thought. He was so excited.

"I'll do everything," I said leaning Jackson back.

It felt so good, I looked down at Jackson. He had a strange look on his face. I could tell he was enjoying it, but he wore a guilty look. But it was so good we couldn't stop. After we finished, we sat there out of breath. I couldn't look him in the eye. We both went into our rooms, not saying a word to each other. When I closed my door, the shame hit harder than anything else. What had I done? There's no way he could ever forgive me for something like this. Nor could I forgive myself. I took advantage of him. Even if I was drunk too, I shouldn't have said it or done it. Tears rushed down my cheeks as my content world with Jackson ended.

I woke up that morning with a raging headache.

"Shit," I said. "I drank too much last night."

As I got out of the bed, faint memories of the night before flushed into my mind. I was scared to leave the room. I was sure Mr. homophobe would punch the lights out of me. But we were both drunk so I hoped he wouldn't remember the night before. I got dressed and took a deep breath. I opened the door slightly and peeped into the hall, then across to Jackson's door. He was still asleep. I quietly closed my door and grabbed my phone, wallet and keys. I opened the door again this time fully and looked around. I rushed down the hall and to the front door. I heard Jackson opening the door as I put my shoes on. I quickly grabbed my other shoe and headphones off the end table and ran out the door only locking our bottom lock. I put on my other shoe as I walked to the end of the hall and into the elevator.

"I gotta call Steph," I thought taking my phone out my pocket.

Steph was my other best friend. I could always come to her whenever I need to talk or just get away from Jackson. I knew she was gonna be pissed when she found out I slept with him. Steph always told me to move out before something I regretted happened.

The phone rang 3 times before she answered, "Hello?"

"Is it alright if I stay a few days at your place?"

"What happened," Steph said annoyance in her voice.

"Um…" it was hard to talk. Sadness sunk in hearing her voice. "I…could I tell you when I get there?"

"Of course, how far away are you?"

"I just left my apartment and I'm getting on the bus."

"Alright, let me hop in the shower and get dressed. I'll talk to you when you get here."

"Okay," I said hanging up.

I put my headphones on, leaned my head on the window and turned my music on loudly.

When I got off the bus, Steph was waiting for me tapping her foot. Her hands folded over her chest.

"Well?" she asked.

I looked at the ground and went to hug her, "I'm an idiot."

I was crying again.

"Hunny, let's go inside," Steph said leading me to her house.

When we got to the door Steph said, "I'll make us some tea and you can tell me."

"I slept with Jackson," I blurted out.

Steph paused as she opened the door.

"What did you say?"

"Leah broke up with him, we were drinking and got really drunk. I sat next to him and he asked me if I was the "f" word, and I just replied what if I was. Then I wasn't thinking straight and asked him to have sex with me. He agreed and we were both hesitant but ended up going through with it. I feel like shit."

I placed my head in my hands.

"Okay let's go in," Steph said pulling my arm.

"It felt great, but I don't think it was worth it, now he won't even speak to me."

"So you tried to talk about it?"

"No, I ran out the house as fast as I could so we wouldn't."

"Normally, you know me, I would have told you to talk it out. But with Jackson, I don't know. He's a different case," Steph said laughing. "When I decided to make the transition, he completely started freaking out and avoided me. We still talk, but he acts weird to this day."

"I don't want us to be awkward around each other."

"I mean the only way is to talk it out."

"I guess," I said nodding. "But maybe in a few days when we both calm down."

"Understandable, but I expect you two to talk it out. And if he doesn't get over it, good riddance. I've been telling you for a while to get over him and find someone better."

"If I could, I would have a long time ago. You know how hard it is for me to get over people. And me and Jackson have lived together for 2 years."

"I understand that Drew," Steph said looking me seriously in the eyes. "If that were me and Randy, I would feel the same way. But in time you would forget him. Just like the others."

Steph smiled and continued, "I'll go get the guest room ready, just relax and wait."

"Okay thank you."

That night I lay there in bed, thinking of what possible outcomes could happen with me and Jackson. But only one seemed realistic. Him punching me and never speaking to me again.

We were both at fault, but I just felt guilty. Maybe because I liked him and there were motives and a reason behind it. Rather than just being horny. But regardless, we had to talk it out sooner or later.

Steph had two guest rooms but always left one open for me. It was my favorite room. It was decorated so beautifully. Randy, Steph's husband was a painter and he painted all the rooms in the house but this one was different. He painted a beautiful landscape. Tall grass lined the bottom quarter of the walls, and a tree on each wall and each wall had different times of day painted. Dawn, afternoon, dusk, and night. When you looked up, you could look through their sky roof as if you were really in nature. I was always calmed when I looked up in bed. I could watch the clouds or look at the stars.

I sat my things down and sat on the recliner. I looked up my mind was clearing as my thoughts of what happened went away. I pulled out my phone. I started texting Jackson where I was, when I remembered this wasn't the time to text him. I needed to wait a little bit.

A week passed, I never texted Jackson and he didn't text me. Usually, Jackson would ask where I was yet this time, not even a text asking if I was okay. He was definitely upset. But it was time to accept my fate. I hugged Steph and said goodbye to her and Randy. And headed home. When I got inside, it was a mess. It was completely trashed, the couch pillows were thrown around, books were on the floor, plates and silverware all over the place. And sitting in the middle was Jackson. He was sitting crisscross, and his head rested in his hands. I was nervous to speak to him and contemplated just leaving the house again. But I knew it was time to face him like an adult.

"Jackson," I said softly. "Are you alright? We should talk about this."

"…"

"I'm really sorry about what happened. We were drunk and I shouldn't have asked you. I'm sorry."

Jackson looked at me, or rather coldly stared, "You leave for a week without saying anything and just come back to apologize?"

"I'm sorry. I know you don't like homosexuals, and what we did…" I trailed off. I couldn't finish what I was going to say. I was so scared and my heart was breaking as I spoke.

I breathed in, "I know you're angry, I just wish that this doesn't change anything between us. And we can stay friends."

"Do you really think we could be friends after having sex? Not even straight relationships can just pretend like nothing happened. And are you really okay with *just* being friends?"

"What?"

"I already knew you liked me. Knew for a long time."

"S-since when," I asked stunned.

"You were really obvious. It was about a year ago. I was on guard. But you didn't and hadn't tried anything, so I relaxed."

"Then why do you keep saying homophobic things if your friend is gay?"

He knew all along and didn't say anything.

Jackson shrugged, "Cause I'm comfortable around you. And you seemed fine with it whenever I would rant."

"Well if we can't just continue how we were," I swallowed deeply. "What do you want to do?"

I already knew his answer, but I needed to hear it for myself.

"I mean, it wasn't just your fault. I also had sex by choice. What was your biggest resolution for this?"

"You punching me..."

"Really?" Jackson said, his tone annoyed. "I'm not some brute."

"I know but you really hate when guys even look at you in a way that's sexual. I did more than that."

"I should punch you for leaving without a word, but not for this. I thought about it rationally the past few days."

"Rational," I mumbled looking around the room.

"That was regret. I felt bad because I knew how you felt about me. I used you when I was feeling down."

"You didn't use me."

"I used you and you used the opportunity to touch me."

"We're kinda beating around the bush on what we want to do," I chuckled quietly.

"I know what you want, hypothetically, and I'm thinking about what I should do," Jackson said holding his chin. "I don't want to make the wrong choice, and we both regret it..."

Jackson stopped and looked at me seriously, "If I decided we should date, how would you react?"

"I would be happy but would think this was either a joke or a horrible dream."

"Why horrible?"

"Because you wake up. Back to reality and end up disappointed."

"And if I ended our friendship and moved out?"

"That's obvious, I would be sad and really regret what I did."

"Same. Well maybe we could go out. As a sort of trial run."

"No way," I said in disbelief.

"I've been thinking about it for a while. You did something awkward while I was working out. It got me thinking what would happen if I did date you and what it would be like. But it was too disturbing, no offense."

"It's okay."

"But over time, I kinda normalized it with you. But just couldn't bring myself to accept it. Then we did what we did. And you left me here alone to think about it. And," he paused and shrugged. "I would like to try it out. But just to let you know in advance, I might not like it after all and want to break up. That's why I said I had two choices I could regret."

"Well we could date, and you see what it's like to date a guy. And if we break up, I wouldn't be mad or anything. At least I got to date you. It'll be easier to get over you."

Jackson smiled, "Then I guess we're dating. I still have a bit of feelings left for Leah though."

"That's fine," I smiled. "But you don't have to force yourself to date me. Not everyone is homosexual and not everyone is straight."

"Well I got it up for you, so it could just be you, or I'm bisexual. I don't know, but worth a try."

Jackson walked over to me and kissed me.

"How was that?" I asked.

"Not bad, I liked it," Jackson smiled leaning in to kiss me again.

I hugged Jackson and closed my eyes. The smell of his cologne was strong, and I loved it. I always wanted to just grab his shirt and bury my face in it. Now I could do that without worrying it was weird or creepy.

"Let's go out to dinner, my treat," Jackson said.

"Okay," I said holding his hand.

We walked out the door and to a local diner. And had an amazing dinner.

"I love you," I said.

"I love you too."

I opened my eyes. The sky was bright, and clouds gently floated above Steph's sky roof. I looked over to see the time, 10 am. I turned back to look outside.

"A dream huh?"

I scoffed before bursting into tears.

"Fuck," I said turning to my side and going under the blanket.

I must have cried for hours. Steph came into the room shouting for me to wake up and talk to Jackson.

"It's already 3pm. You need to get up and go home. I love you and you're always welcome. But you need to fix this."

"I know," I said. "I had a dream we made up and started dating. I was so happy."

"Aw hunny," Steph said hugging me.

"But I need to face him. It might not turn out the same way, but I can still try."

"That's right," Steph said.

I said bye for real and headed to my apartment.

When I got back, the apartment was clean. Maybe even cleaner than when I left. Jackson always cleaned when he was angry. It was his way of clearing his mind.

"Jackson?" I asked walking fully inside.

It was really quiet, I thought he might still be at work. I poured myself a glass of water and relaxed on our couch. I breathed in and saw something white in the corner of my eye. On the end table was a set of keys and a letter addressed to me. It was from Jackson.

It read:

Dear Drew,

I'm really sorry about what happened last night. We were both really drunk. I wish I could leave it there. But I just can't share an apartment with someone who's clearly gay. It sucks, we were great friends. After what happened, I doubt I could look at you the same. It's best we just separate now before we ruin our friendship further. I'll be out of here by the time you get back tonight. I already found a place to stay. You can keep all the furniture, even in my room.

I wish you the best,
Jackson.

I rushed to Jackson's room and opened the door. The closet was cleared out and his bedding gone. Shocked, I slumped to the floor, my mouth agape. A tear rolled down my cheek. He actually left. This whole time I thought he was here brooding over it. He just packed up and hit the road. That faint hope that we could have become more than friends had fizzled out. I lay down on the floor in his room, it was all over. A thoughtless action led to such a huge mistake.

It's been a few weeks, I saw Jackson around campus with his friends, but we never talked again. I'm still in love with him. But over time I'll heal. And find someone worth loving and believes I'm worth loving.

A Night of Rain

I couldn't get her out of my mind.

One Night in the Rain

I was a screenwriter at the time with numerous hits. Most people knew me as this amazing successful writer and convincing actor. But I had a side few knew about. I was a "player". I slept around with many women. I didn't care about calling them back or about their broken hearts when I ran into them again. I was living a wild life. I drank until sunrise. I had affairs with housewives that couldn't stand their husbands, the experimental college student, the closeted girlfriend, and many more. And still made my deadlines.

On a rainy night, while at a bar with few people, I met a woman. Her name was Annalise. She was gorgeous. Her beautiful brown skin and long curly black hair. I couldn't take my eyes off her. I slid out of my stool and walked over to her.

"Hi, I'm Adrienne," I said holding my hand out.

With a wide smile she said, "I know who you are. You're the infamous Adrienne. You sleep with women claiming you love them and never calling them back. You're also Juliet Morris, known for all of your movies."

"You know a lot about me," I chuckled.

"Word gets around," she said, her tongue slid sensually across her bottom lip as she glanced over my body.

I bit my lip and said, "Well since you know all of that, I guess you know what I'm interested in."

Annalise laughed, "You are so cute, but what makes you think I want you?"

She really was a sight for sore eyes. Even her laugh was enough to get me going.

"You would have turned me down a long time ago. Yet…you're still entertaining me."

Annalise smiled and rolled her eyes, "You got me."

"How about heading to my place?"

"Sure thing," Annalise grabbed her purse and stood up.

She was shorter than me, which was a great quality. She was skinny, but her chest and hips were full. She was my type in every aspect. I stuck my elbow out and she looped her arm around mine and smiled.

When we got to my condo, I pulled Annalise to me and kissed her passionately. Annalise wrapped her arms around me, and I carried her to bed. It was amazing. She was so sexy and was great in bed. The best I ever slept with. But it was something about her that had me wanting more.

As we lay there, I turned to her and said, "We should definitely do this again."

"Really?" she asked amused. "You never sleep with the same person twice."

"Hm, you're special," I said running my hand through her curls.

"Do you say that to everyone?"

"I mean it with you."

"And I guess you want my number too."

"Obviously," I said kissing her forehead. "How am I gonna contact you?"

Annalise turned to me and started fiddling with the necklace I was wearing.

"I think," she said. "You have a kink, pretending you like someone and wanting their number just to block them."

"I don't have a kink. The women I slept with were too clingy and possessive. Would you want to deal with someone like that?"

"No, but you don't just ghost them. Let'em down nicely."

"I see that. But it is what it is. I wouldn't do that to you though."

"So sweet of you," Annalise said sarcastically.

I looked at the clock, it was 3 am.

"Well, there's a little more time," I said rolling onto her. "Let's go one more round."

Annalise laughed as I kissed her neck.

The next morning I felt refreshed. I hadn't had anything so amazing, not for a long time. I looked over to see Annalise one more time before work, but she was gone. My heart sank a little. She never gave me her number.

I rolled out of bed and headed to the door before seeing a note on her side of the bed.

Adrienne,
Sorry I couldn't stay longer X
Here's my number, call me anytime. XOXO

I rushed to my phone and saved her number before I could forget. Though, she wasn't forgettable.

That night I went back to the bar I met Annalise, hoping I would run into her again. I looked around the bar quickly not to be obvious. She wasn't there. Disappointed, I sat down in my usual spot and ordered Tequila. I browsed my selection of women, but none could compare to Annalise. They were all dull. Dull smiles, dull hair, everything was dull. Before I wasted time on those women, I figured I could get Annalise to come over one more time.

"Hey gorgeous," I texted her. "Want to have a go at my place?"

"Sorry," she replied. "I already found someone for the night."

"Next time."

"Seriously," I mumbled setting my phone down.

She was obviously stunning so finding someone wouldn't be hard. But that left me to find someone incomparable. I skimmed the bar again and saw a woman in a red dress sitting alone. She was sexy. We made eye contact and she smiled. I took that as my cue and approached her.

"You look stunning," I said extending my hand. "I'm Adrienne."

"Leanne," she softly took my hand.

We talked for maybe an hour, before I invited her to my condo. She was open to anything. She wasn't necessarily lesbian, as she put it. But she found women more attractive than men. We reached my place and her red dress was off. Looking at her naked, just wasn't the same. Annalise messed me up. No woman I was with would satisfy my hunger. Leanne and I had sex, but it didn't feel right. It felt average. Nothing worth trying again. Leanne didn't stay the night and I was glad she didn't.

Over the next week, I texted Annalise, but she never responded. It was frustrating. She agreed to seeing me again. But never had time, not even enough to reply. I came to the bar again, hoping to meet Annalise. I walked in slowly and looked around. By the bar, I saw a woman with the same beautiful curls as Annalise. I smiled and casually walked to the bar and sat a couple stools away.

"I'll have a Margaretta," I said handing the bartender a $20.

Pretending to not notice her, I looked at the selection of alcohol. I turned to look in her direction. I glanced at Annalise who was smiling at me and looked back to the alcohol.

I did a double take and said, "Hey, I didn't notice that was you. How have you been?"

"Good. It's nice to come here and relax every so often," she rested her head on her hand. "How about you?"

"Fabulous now that I've seen you."

Annalise laughed, "You did not just pull that line."

"I did, because it's true," I said taking her other hand. "You really are unforgettable. I want you."

"Yeah?" she smiled. "And what exactly would having me entail?"

"Being my lover," I said looking her in the eyes.

"Lover?" she repeated astonished. "You really should find another term. I didn't even think love was in your vocabulary."

"It is, but I don't fall in love."

"But the definition of lover is a romantic relationship, which neither of us is looking for."

"It's also defined as a sexual relationship. But how about friends with benefits?"

"That sounds a little more appropriate," she said smiling.

"And your answer?"

Annalise pursed her lips, "Hmm, why not. But only for a little while."

Me and Annalise met every night. I was addicted. You could say we were lovers. I didn't sleep with anyone else. She was all I needed and the only one I could be with.

"Say," Annalise said walking to my kitchen. "I've been thinking. I really don't know much about you nor you me. Maybe tonight, we could just sit and talk?"

I wrapped my arms around her and started kissing her neck, "I didn't think we had to?"

"I'm serious," Annalise said breaking away from me. "You really think it's okay to just sleep with someone for so long and not know their favorite color?"

"I never thought about it. You're the first person I've slept with more than once."

"Well, I don't think I'm interested tonight, or ever, until we've known enough facts about each other."

I rolled my eyes and sat at the dining table, "Have a seat. Let's get to know each other."

Annalise smiled, "Now we're getting somewhere."

"So how old are you?" I asked.

"You don't even know how old I am," she scoffed.

"Come on, age doesn't matter. Besides, like you know how old I am."

"You're 32."

I paused, "Well I'm famous so it's easy to know my age. And I just don't think about those things."

"I still care enough to remember."

"I'm sorry," I said giving in. "I won't forget if you tell me."

"I'm 21."

"Man, I feel like such a creep being with someone so young."

"Yeah because you haven't slept with anyone 18," she laughed.

"I haven't actually."

Annalise gave me a look, "You're not actually lying right now are you?"

"No. Or at least I didn't know they were 18. Or purposely going after them because they were."

"Uh huh," she said standing up to pour some wine. "Virgins, you really didn't have a conscious."

"I did. But if someone wants to lose their virginity to me, I'm not going to say no. Would you?"

"Yes I would. Unless we were serious, I wouldn't just snatch it and block them."

I shrugged, "To each their own. If someone wants me that's on them. Not me."

Annalise shook her head, "I'm surprised no one's tried to kill you."

"Maybe they have," I laughed.

Annalise began to laugh along, "You're so obnoxious."

I stood up and walked to Annalise who was smiling and biting the rim of her wineglass. My body close to hers.

Towering over her I said, "Who are you calling obnoxious."

"You," she said standing on her tiptoes.

I bit my lips and picked up Annalise, "That's it."

Annalise squealed as I carried her to my bed.

After we had sex, I watched her sleep. She was so beautiful. I couldn't describe how I felt. I ran my hand through her hair and dozed off to sleep.

By morning she was already gone. The day sluggishly went by. It was boring and uneventful. I wanted to see Annalise so bad, but it was our off day. That night, I lay in bed staring at the ceiling. I reached for my phone and rolled over. It was late, but I wanted to talk to Annalise.

"I miss you," I texted her.

No response.

"She must be sleeping," I thought before dozing off.

I checked my phone the moment I woke up. Hoping Annalise would text me. But still nothing. I sighed and sent a "good morning" text and lay in bed. I finished my deadline so I could stay in bed as long as I wanted.

I sent her another text, "Are you coming over tonight?"

Still no response.

As the day went by, I didn't hear a peep from Annalise. It was weird not hearing from her, she was the type to respond to texts right away. It was rare for her to not answer a text. Annalise told me once, she responded to things in a timely manner. Her OCD was having notifications just waiting on her phone. I found that a cute aspect of hers. I flopped down on my couch and sighed. I assumed she wasn't coming over, and I got disappointed even more. I had no desire to go out. There was no point, when the only person I could be with and enjoy it, was Annalise. I turned on a movie.

A few weeks passed and I never got any contact from Annalise, I was worried. Maybe something bad happened to her? Or what if she lost interest in me. I was a lot older than her. Younger people lost interest fast. Day after day I thought about her. What she was doing, where she was and if she was with someone new. I became frustrated. I couldn't understand why Annalise was on my mind so much recently.

I was heading to bed early when I thought, maybe she would be there tonight. I quickly got dressed and headed for the bar.

When I got there, it was crowded. I pushed my way to the counter and sat down.

"Shit," I said to the bartender. "Why's it so busy today?"

"I have no idea," he said laughing. "But no complaints, more tips for me."

"Damn, ain't that the truth," I said browsing the tables.

"Looking for someone?"

"Yeah, I don't know if you remember her, but Annalise?"

"No, but I know how popular you are, so it's surprising she didn't give you her number."

"No, she did. She just hasn't responded to my texts. Which is also rare."

"Wow, the Adrienne having someone ignore her. Guess, you can't have everyone."

"Yeah, but she's the only one I want."

"So you're in love with her."

"Love?" I replied almost choking on my drink. "No, I'm not the loving type."

"That sounds like you like her."

"I like the sex, not her."

"Mm, sure," he said walking away to get a customer's drink.

"Like? Love? You gotta be kidding me," I thought. "How could I like someone just from a few times?"

I gazed into my drink, rubbing the side. I was spacing out. But then it hit me. From the beginning, before talking to her I was mesmerized. Was I really in love with her? I never loved someone. That wasn't my thing, to be tied down by one woman. Maybe I confused love for lust? As I spaced out, I noticed a figure sitting down next to me. I turned my head as they sat down. It was Annalise. Her eyes were so beautiful and bright. Her smile took my breath away.

"It sure is crowded tonight," she said waving to the bartender.

I smiled, "Yeah, it's crazy tonight."

"I liked the aesthetic it had. That quiet, nighttime bar with smooth jazz playing softly."

"Now it's loud and obnoxious."

"Exactly. Not to mention it's impossible to find people."

"You? Unlikely, you could walk up to anyone in this bar and you'd have them."

Annalise laughed, "That's sweet of you, but I meant friends."

"That too," I said regretting every word.

"Tell me," Annalise said turning her body fully towards me. "Is sex really all you think about?"

"Not anymore," I said looking down. "I had a change of heart."

"Ooh," Annalise said mockingly. "What? Did someone catch your eye?"

"You could say that."

"Wait, really? THE Adrienne falling in love? The world must be ending."

I chuckled, "Yeah, it's pretty crazy. I hadn't noticed until tonight. But looking now, even I have to admit it."

"She must be something else if she can snag you."

"Can I ask you something? It's not that big a deal, but why didn't you respond to my texts?"

"Did you text me?" Annalise asked grabbing her phone. "Oh…sorry, I don't go on my phone that much anymore."

"It's fine. So do you want to hang out at my place?"

"And do what exactly?" Annalise asked laughing. "You should maybe try settling down with the girl you like. Rather than going to bed with just anyone."

Annalise stood up.

"I should probably get going. There's no way I can find the right person in this crowd, and it's too loud to relax."

I quickly stood up, "How about I walk you out then?"

"Nah, I'll be fine."

I followed her anyways, I didn't want to part just yet. I had a feeling I wouldn't see her again.

"It's better to be safe than sorry right?"

"That's true," she said not looking back.

I quickened my pace so I could walk side to side. But when we left the bar, Annalise stopped and turned to me.

"You really don't need to walk me to my car."

"I know, I just want to spend a little more time with you is all."

"Why?"

I paused. I almost blurted out I liked her. I had to assess if that were the smart thing to do. But at this point, it was my only option.

"Because you're the woman I like."

Annalise froze and stared at me.

"I didn't notice at first but the pass few weeks have been torment. I can't be with anyone else but you."

"Do you really expect me to believe that?" she asked frustrated.

"I mean, I wouldn't just tell you that if I didn't mean it."

"You wouldn't," she repeated. "Tell that to the hundreds of women you led on for years."

"That was different. I—"

"How so?" she interrupted. "Because it's exactly the same. Lying to women and saying you love them. Then not giving a shit when you hurt them. How can I trust you."

"I know, I did some fucked up things. But I—I really do feel this way. I just told you in the bar and didn't mention a word it was you."

"Then why tell me now?"

"I had this feeling I wouldn't see you after tonight. I couldn't bear the thought."

"And you were right," she said stepping closer. "You really think I could just sit there and let you tell me you loved someone. You of all people shouldn't have the right. Not the right to say, 'I love you.' Not the right to love and definitely not the right to be accepted."

Annalise's words cut deep. I couldn't fathom why she was so angry? What I did with other women shouldn't affect my relationship with her.

"That's a bit harsh, don't you think?" I asked awkwardly laughing.

"No, not to someone like you. Now goodbye."

Annalise spun around and ran to her car.

"Wait," I said following her. I grabbed her arm. "Please, please don't go. I'm sorry to all the women I hurt. I'll go and find all of them and apologize. Please don't leave."

Annalise didn't look at me, but she stopped trying to leave.

"Please, maybe you don't feel that way about me. But you wouldn't get so offended if you didn't."

"I have a reason," she mumbled. "You don't even remember me."

"Remember you?" I asked.

"Yes, you don't even know who I am. Yet you stand here saying you love me."

"I know who you are," I said leaning over to see her face.

"You don't," she forced out.

Annalise turned to me and looked me in the eyes.

"You don't remember me. My name isn't 'Annalise.' You can't say you love me, when you don't remember breaking my heart," she screamed, tears were rolling down her face.

"What?" I asked taken aback. "You…you were one of the women?"

"Yes," she said. "And like every one of them, for no reason you said you loved me."

I kept quiet.

"It was three years ago at this bar. I was 18 and nervous. Afraid to leave the counter but I wanted to try new things. And you approached me. Saying I was beautiful, and it was love at first sight. And like an idiot I fell for it."

She continued, "You took me to your place and kissed me. I told you it was my first time and that I was scared. And maybe you said it to make me less nervous but lied that it was also your first time. After we had sex, you told me you loved me and wanted to see me again. But that was a lie. You didn't accept my calls or answer my texts. When I saw you again at this bar, you were already with another woman. I went after you, but you pretended to not know me. After that, you sent me a text telling me to 'leave you the fuck alone' and I assumed, blocked my number."

"I'm so sorry," I said shocked. I couldn't place her anywhere, but something in me knew she wasn't lying.

"You're probably trying to figure out why you can't remember me. It's because I'm not the same ugly nerdy girl with glasses. I was really damaged by how you treated me. And I blamed my looks. I got this whole make over and went back. And sure enough, there you were, swooping in for another night. And to top it off, after all the work I put into myself, you didn't even remember I was the same person you told to fuck off."

I didn't know what to say to her, what could I say to her? I was a complete ass, and nothing I did would redeem myself. I never really looked at how my actions hurt others. And here I was, staring at a woman whose life I ruined. Who changed herself just to suit me. My heart was hurting. Seeing her cry, broke me even more.

"And after all this," she said. "I still love you. I couldn't break it off like I planned to."

I embraced 'Annalise,' my face resting on her head, "I'm so so sorry. Nothing I do will ever negate what I did. But I promise you, if you give me another chance, I will never hurt you again."

I continued, "Yes you weren't my first and I'm sorry I said you were. But you are my first love. I love you, regardless of who you are, or who you were. Only the woman standing in front of me now."

'Annalise' wrapped her arms around me and rested her face on my chest.

"I'm stupid for forgiving you, but just promise me this is real."

"It is. I'm serious about you."

I lifted 'Annalise's' head and kissed her passionately. Maybe it was her love that made this feel nice, but I never wanted to part from her. I took 'Annalise' to my condo and we made love all night.

We lay cuddling in bed, I never felt so happy in my life. But there was still one problem.

"You know, you still haven't told me your actual name."

She laughed, "Elizabeth."

"I think that's way prettier than Annalise," I said kissing her forehead.

"Wow, that's not offensive."

"No, it's not. Your name isn't Annalise."

"It's my middle name."

"Really? Well Annalise is a pretty name. But Elizabeth is beautiful."

"That's so cheesy."

Since then, Elizabeth and I got married, and have lived happily for 8 years. We're considering children, but I'm not ready yet. And I really meant what I said back then, I went through my list of contacts and apologized to every woman I slept with. It was brutal, but in the end, they all deserved closure.

A Day of Rain

He was a lot bigger than me. He was rough and grumpy. I was quiet and gentle. We were best friends.

I wish I didn't have to go. Will we be friends after I'm gone? Will he still like me?

Memories

My parents were both high status people. My father was a doctor and my mother was a renowned professor for some study of the human body. My father and mother were offered jobs in America relatively close to each other. And so, my family and I moved to the United States. I was 8 and my English was terrible. No one in the new school district we moved to, knew Japanese. Luckily my father was American, and along the way, taught me and my brother English. But I was so scared. I wanted to play with the other kids, but they wouldn't understand me.

I sat by myself on the swings, it was getting dark. All the children were leaving with their parents. I lived across the street from the park, so I didn't have to go. I felt so alone, I softly swung my feet that dangled slightly above the ground. I was going to cry, when the kid next door busted out the door. He was clearly angry.

"I don't care," he shouted as he closed the door.

I stared at him and we made eye contact. I quickly looked down so he wouldn't yell at me. I peeped at him and saw he was walking to me. I was scared. I always saw movies where Black people would fight, rob, and kill people. I didn't want that to happen to me. I clenched the chains on the swing and squeezed my eyes closed.

"Can you believe them?" he asked frustrated. He plopped down on the swing next to me. "They took away my video games cause they said I don't play outside enough."

His voice was raspy and high pitched. I looked at him. I was better at speaking English, but he was speaking too fast.

"My English is not good," I said waving my hand. "I'm sorry. You are speaking too fast."

"Really?" he asked. Speaking slower he said, "Where are you from? China?"

"No, I'm…uh…Japanese."

"Ooh," he said nodding his head. "That was my second guess."

I nodded, I was still scared but I didn't know how to walk away or talk to him.

"I'm Michael," he said.

"Seijirou."

"'Seijirou,'" he repeated. "That's a cool name, I like it."

"Thanks," I mumbled.

"I know a little Japanese," he said swinging. "My brother is an English teacher in Japan. He teaches me words every now and then. Konnichiwa, ohayo, gohan, yasumi. It's a pretty fun language to learn."

I watched him swing and asked, "How come you're not hitting me?"

"What?" he asked so shocked he almost fell off. He stopped himself from swinging and said, "Why would I hit you? Are you used to being bullied?"

"Aren't Black people violent?"

"No," he looked offended. "Where did you hear nonsense like that?"

"I see it in movies and TV shows. And I sometimes heard it from my neighbors."

"Those are just movies. That's not real. They're actors. Not every Black person is violent," he said standing up. "I didn't think any stereotypes about you. But you thought that I was going to hurt you."

"But you thought I was from China."

"That's not the same. I was just guessing 'cause I didn't know. Yours was racist."

He walked away.

"Where are you going?" I shouted.

"I don't want to play with you anymore."

Michael walked back to his house. As he was going inside, he looked at me once more, shook his head, and turned inside. I felt bad, I didn't think that would hurt his feelings. At the same time, my mom was calling me to come home. When I got inside dinner was on the table. At home we spoke Japanese. Unless it was time to practice English.

"Mom," I asked in Japanese.

"Yes?" she replied.

"I have a question. So I met this Black kid at the park, and I asked him why he wasn't violent, and he got upset and said he didn't want to play with me anymore. I don't understand why he was so angry."

"You asked him that?" Dad asked.

"Yes, I was scared that he would hurt me like they do in movies. But he didn't, so I asked him why he was different from other Black people. And he got mad."

"Because that wasn't an appropriate thing to say," he said. "You can't judge people by their looks. Not every Black person is like how they appear on TV. That's just make believe."

"I feel really bad," I said pushing my food around.

"You should, and the next time you see him, apologize."

"Yes dad," I said.

After dinner, I sat on my bedroom floor and continued to unpack. I missed my chance to make a friend. I was so stupid. I pulled out my curtains and stood up.

"I should hang these up," I thought.

I walked to the window and saw Michael sitting by his window on a video game. I pushed open my window and waved to get his attention. He rolled his eyes and opened his window.

"Yes," he asked obviously frustrated.

"I'm sorry about what I said earlier. I was being stupid and didn't understand the difference between movies and real life. I'm sorry. I really hope we can be friends. You would be my first friend since coming here."

He stood silently, then smiled, "Alright. I also just moved here. Two months ago and haven't made a friend."

I was excited, my first friend.

"Do you want to come over and play games?"

"I can't," I said. "My mom's mad I didn't unpack yet."

"How long have you lived here?"

"A month."

"A month?!" he shouted. "Why did you wait?"

"It's boring, but I'm almost done."

"I wish my mom would be that cool. I had to unpack the next morning."

"I think because it's a long move from Japan to here. They don't want to stress me out more."

"That makes sense. I would help you if I could. But I doubt my mom, or your mom would let me."

"I'll ask," I said running away from the window. I raced to the living room where they were.

"Done already?" Dad asked.

"No, but I made up with the kid and we're friends."

"That's great but how did you?" Mom asked.

"He lives next door. I saw him by the window and said sorry."

"Good job," Dad said.

"I wanted to know if it was okay if he helped me finish unpacking?"

"It's getting kind of late," Mom said.

"It is," Dad replied.

"I'm almost done, please it'll go way faster with him."

Mom and Dad looked at each other.

"Alright," Dad said. "As long as his parents are okay with it."

"Yes," I shouted and ran back to my window.

"What did your parents say?"

"As long as it's okay with your parents."

"My mom's okay with it."

"Really, yes!"

"I'll head over now," Michael said jumping up and running away from the window.

When he came over, I introduced him to my parents. We had so much fun, I couldn't even believe I was scared of him. He was nicer than anyone else I met. Every day we played together. We didn't go to the same school. He went to an all boy's school and I went to the public school.

As the months went by, we grew closer and closer. I was in love with him half a year after meeting him. Every moment was precious to me. But life at home was becoming worse. My parents grew apart and were always arguing. They eventually agreed to divorce two years after moving there. My father took custody of my brother, and my mother had custody of me. She planned to move back to Japan, she willingly gave the house to my father, just so she could at least have one of her kids.

I was upset, I ran to Michael's house, when they told me.

"Michael, it's horrible! I have to move away."

"What? Why?"

"My parents are getting divorced, and my mother wants to go back to Japan."

"Japan?" Michael yelled. "Why can't she stay here?"

"I don't know, I wish I could stay."

"Me too," Michael said. "When do you leave?"

"Tomorrow."

"Do you want to hang out at my house? Since this will be the last time?"

I nodded and followed him inside.

When we reached his room, I couldn't hold my tears any longer.

"I don't want to leave," I wailed.

Michael hugged me, "Me either."

I figured that was going to be the last time I saw him, I had to tell him how I felt.

"I like you," I mumbled.

"I like you too."

"No, I mean I like you like you."

"Really?" Michael said shocked. "Since when?"

"Like, a few months ago. That's why it sucks even more that I have to leave."

"I like you too," Michael said looking down. "But it feels kind of useless to say because we won't be able to see each other."

"Yeah, but at least we said something."

"That's true…" he said. "How about we make a promise. When we get older, we'll marry each other."

I smiled, "Deal."

I leaned in and kissed Michael. He paused and started freaking out.

"That was my first kiss," he said covering his mouth.

"Mine too."

We smiled and giggled. My father called me back to the house to pack. I gave Michael one last hug and left.

The next day, we finished loading our car. I looked at Michael's window. He was standing there watching. I smiled and waved. Michael waved back and my mother and I drove away.

My mother and I moved in with my grandma until my mom was back on her feet. We moved to a rural town, so I had to make friends all over again. The only thing that kept me motivated was our promise.

It was hard being away from Michael. Over time, Michael stopped contacting me. I emailed daily but he never responded. After a while, I figured he must have gotten a new email and lost my contact. I didn't worry too much because my dad still lived in the house next to him. I could always see him if I ever got to see my dad and Ryuichi again.

Years went by and still no contact from Michael. I knew deep down, he must have forgotten me. Still, I just couldn't forget him. He meant the world to me. I would have done anything to see him again. Even for a little bit.

But my wish came sooner than expected. And not the way I wanted it to. It was the start of my first year in high school. I was late coming home because my club meeting ran longer than planned. When I came home, the police were waiting with my neighbor. She pointed at me and the cops came over. My mother had been in an accident. She was pronounced dead at the scene. My neighbor told me my mother was worried that I hadn't contacted her. She decided to pick me up from school. I had no family in Japan that I knew of. My grandma passed away years ago, and as far as I knew, mother was an only child.

So I contacted my dad, and he flew me to America. Ryuichi blamed me for her death, and he wasn't wrong. I blamed myself as well. But he resented me, and never spoke to me again. Seeing Michael again, was the only thing helping me through it.

I was so nervous. I would finally see Michael again. I asked to be enrolled at the private school he attended. And I didn't expect to be in the same class as him. I was so scared, I didn't know what to do, and like an idiot, I ignored him. But I was glad he spoke to me first.

~~~

When I came to, I was in the hospital. My head was hurting and the room was spinning. I was in a lot of pain. I winced as I sat up. My vision was blurry. I looked to my side and saw someone sleeping there. I squinted until my vision came back. It was Michael. I was so confused, what happened? I couldn't focus but I needed to recall what happened. I closed my eyes. I remembered telling Michael how I felt, and then leaving when he hurt me. I couldn't see in the rain. I just remembered a loud sound and a light growing bigger as it came near me. Was I hit by a car? I was stunned. I felt like I was hit by a truck when he rejected me, but never thought it would happen to me.

I looked back to Michael, he was crying. I placed my hand on his head and gently stroked his hair.

Michael opened his eyes, "Seiji...I..."
~~~

He continued, "I'm so sorry. This is all my fault. I shouldn't have said what I said. I didn't mean it."

Michael was crying so hard. I could hear him struggling to breathe.

"It's okay," I said. "It's not your fault. I should have been more careful."

"I thought I lost you," he said. "Seeing all of this. You getting hit by a truck, being in this hospital, it made me remember the feelings I had for you back then. I don't know if you'll forgive me. But, will you give me another chance."

I chuckled, "You're just saying that because I almost died."

"It's true," he shouted. "I love you so much. When you moved away back then, I was so hurt, I blocked out memories of you. That was the only way I could continue."

I sat quietly and then smiled, "I'll give it one more shot. But you have a lot of making up to do."

Michael smiled so wide. I was amazed anyone could smile like that. He stood up and hugged me.

"Thank you, I love you so much."

"Me too," I said my eyes closed. "I love you too."

Afterwards

If you made it this far, thank you for reading *A Day of Rain*! I hope you liked it. This was the very first novel I started writing. I was in 8th grade. I was really fascinated with LGBT romance novels, one of my favorite American novels (I believe it's American) is *Am I Blue?*. I wanted to write one myself, but it was hard to just write one story, so I wrote two and just didn't know where to go from there. I stopped writing for years and went back to it my junior year of high school. I popped in and out of this book with another story idea. Then I decided I wanted to finish this story. And as I rung in the new year of 2020. I finally finished this book.

It was quite a struggle writing this. I don't quite understand all of the hardship LGBT+ community experiences. So I wrote this from an outside stand point. I live in a relatively liberal city, so it's okay to say you're gay. Or at least I think it is. I just always said I was pansexual when someone asked my sexuality and a good majority in my high school and college were and are open about who they like. That doesn't count for everyone of course, and definitely not when it comes to family. But I wanted to have an equal level of happiness and reality. I didn't want to write all of my stories with disapproval to being gay or trans. Only where it seemed fit. Plus I just love writing sad stories.

I hope that you, the reader, enjoyed these stories. At least one! PLEASE! Lol. And I apologize if any of these stories resemble what you're going through and I hope if it does, it gets better or is better.

I would say, The Library, Unrequited Love, One Night in the Rain and the first story, A Day of Rain, are my favorites.

The Library, I actually originally had a happy ending planned. But as I was writing it, I remember another story I'm writing. I don't want to spoil the story but I thought about how that could play in. I thought about Angel's name, the time I mentioned Heaven and nirvana. And decided to run with it. I had too many stories with happy endings, I needed to fix the ratio a bit. Unrequited Love was the same way. I thought that was too unrealistic the first way and decided to add a little heart break.

One Night in the Rain was the first lesbian story I wrote. I didn't quite know how to write it.

Because I guess, I've never been a "player". And that was another one I changed. Originally, Annalise was supposed to be hired to break Adrienne's heart. So she could get a taste of her own medicine. I was going to have it end with Adrienne never seeing her again. But then I thought, there should be some kind of personal gain for why Annalise would want to get revenge. Not just teaching her a lesson for others but getting back at her for breaking her heart.

A Day of Rain (the first story) was written in the style of Yaoi or BL (Boy's Love). I was young so I can't necessarily explain all the details on why I wrote it. I just loved BL novels and manga so much, I wanted to create one myself. It just developed into more than just BL. And I watched a few anime stories that involved school dorms and some manga with all boy schools. I just had the idea and wrote it. When I was fixing my grammar, I noticed I wrote this story pretty depressing. It was still a nice story, I hope. But A Day of Rain and The "New" Kid, were both written in reference to BL/Yaoi. I was going to go more in depth with The "New" Kid but I couldn't remember the idea I had years ago. Something along the lines of Seiji and Ryuichi both fighting over Michael, but didn't want to.

I'd love to go into more detail about the other stories, but I don't want to put my interpretation of how things ended and why they happened out there. I'm curious to know how you interpreted a story or the stories.

Again, thank you for reading A Day of Rain, and for reading the Afterward. I hope you liked it.

—A.J. Hughes

About the Author

A Day of Rain is A.J.'s second book following *A Walk on the Other Side*. Released in 2018.

A.J. Hughes lives in Madison, WI. with her adorable cat Fatty. She loves to read Manga. Her passions are music, writing, languages and art. Her hope is to create amazing novels for readers all over the world to enjoy.